SUGAR AND
SPICE FANTASY
ROMANCE

VIOLET FIELDS & MIDNIGHT MOUNTAINS

ASTRID VAIL

Copyright

Violet Fields & Midnight Mountains

Any resemblance to actual persons, living or dead, events, or locales is entirely coincidental.

Cover Art by Miblart

Edited by nicegirlnaughtyedits

ISBN

eBook: 978-1-958641-41-5

Paperback: 978-1-958641-42-2

Content Warning: explicit language, spicy scenes between two consenting adults, strained parental relationships, and slight violence.

Human Generated Work: This author does not engage in the usage of AI, nor do they grant permission for AI to use their works.

Human Authored™, Reg #: 8391100, https://authorsguild.org/human

Contents

Before Reading

Violet Fields & Midnight Mountains is a full-length ADULT fantasy romance adventure which includes adult language and spicy scenes.
It is the first book in the Sugar and Spice Fantasy Romance series.
All books are standalones within an interconnected fantasy world.
Content Warning: explicit language, spicy scenes between two consenting adults, strained parental relationships, and slight violence.
Spicy Scenes:
There are *two* spicy scenes within this book.
They do use very explicit language.
I have provided the chapters in which those scenes can be found, below in case you are uncomfortable reading such scenes, and want to skip them or just don't want to read them in public.

A Fork in the Road

THE ANNOYING HUM OF a fly brought Zaharra into wakefulness as she slapped at the insect. She opened her eyes against the glare of the sun and wiped at the sweat dripping down her brow.

It was insanely hot for this time of the year, and Zaharra had sought shelter under a patch of sheltering trees that grew prevalent on the plains. This patch of trees, in particular, sported a large rock that produced just enough shade from the sweltering heat and, in her case, to take a quick nap behind.

It also marked the fork in the road Zaharra was traveling on.

Left led to the Whispering Bluffs and the Nebula Isles. Right led to the Violet Plains and the Midnight Mountains.

The hum of the fly was back, and Zaharra slapped at it again before using the side of the boulder to get to her feet. Grabbing her travel bag, she shaded her eyes and glanced at the sun. It sat high in the cloudless blue sky, having barely moved since she had closed her eyes.

Stupid fly had woken her up from her nap way too early.

But it didn't matter.

She had laid down to rest her feet from her travel and to quiet her anxious mind.

She had only succeeded in one of the two.

Part of her was excited to be headed home after the months she had been away. She missed the bustling town she had grown up in. She missed her best friend, Meerek, and her brothers. She missed her father, his baking, and the way he always brought order and cleanliness to the chaos of their home. She missed her mother's tight-lipped smile, and her barking orders when the young women in her defense classes didn't follow through with the various kicks and punches.

But another part gnawed at her stomach like a starving dog on a bone. Anxiety wove its way through her mind and body, and Zaharra closed her eyes, making herself take a few long, deep breaths.

She was desperately trying to convince herself not to spiral. To tell herself not to be an anxious, nervous wreck.

Her internal self-talk wasn't working, though. Her stomach continued to knot as her mind tried to figure out how she was going to tell her mother she had failed.

That, in the end, it didn't matter how hard she trained, how hard she studied, or even that she was a damn legacy, her family name gracing the queen's hall for the last three generations.

Her mother was going to be so disappointed, and Zaharra hated disappointing her.

She was supposed to be coming back from the queen's city, from her rite of passage into womanhood with good news, not utter disappointment.

The rite of passage was a system built for anyone with orcish blood, between the age of twenty and twenty-five, to come to the city and officially step into adulthood. It was a time of wonder, of learning, and being tested in skills to determine their next steps in life.

Zaharra opened her eyes and shook her head before grabbing her travel bag. Slinging it over her shoulder, she shifted towards the fork in the road leading towards the Violet Plains.

Towards home.

Biting her lip, she glanced to the right, then over her shoulder.

She could always go back to the city, a little voice in the back of her head whispered.

Demand to be retested. Go through it all again.

But in the end, the results would be the same.

No, what mattered now was that she went home and broke the news to her parents. Then figure out what she was supposed to do with the rest of her life.

Her feet dragged, kicking up dust from the road, and she blamed her sluggish gait on the fact she had been traveling for the last three days. Not because she was trying to delay the inevitable.

That she, her mother's only daughter, had somehow failed at becoming the one thing she was raised from birth to be. That she would not be continuing the family tradition of becoming part of the orc queen's personal guard.

All the training and all the late nights studying had been for nothing. It didn't matter that she was proficient in knives, swords, longbow, short bow, and everything in between. It didn't matter that she had physically run circles around more seasoned warriors. It didn't matter. Nothing mattered but what the queen herself decided in the end.

And her decision was to not allow Zaharra into her personal guard.

The annoying voice in the back of her head gnawed at her once again, calling her out for being a failure to her entire bloodline.

It told her to turn around and run the other way.

Instead, Zaharra picked up her pace.

Her walk turned into a jog.

She would not run away from her problems.

No, she would face them head on.

A bustling town surrounded by fields of swaying grassland, dotted with violet flowers, greeted Zaharra as she crossed the final hill that led home. She didn't slow her pace, instead letting bewildered townsfolk stare at her as she jogged down the main street. She could see her family's farm to the right and directed her feet down the familiar path. Squinting towards the fields, she chuckled under her breath as a herd of sheared vysha came into view.

Vysha was a hardy breed, known for their ability to withstand the strong winds and storms that swept across the plains during the summer and winter months. They normally sported long brown coats, except in the summer months. Zaharra huffed, suppressing her laughter as she thought about her brothers wrangling up the vysha without her this year and getting them into the shearing quarters.

To Zaharra, wrangling the vysha, especially the naughty ones who always managed to escape, was second nature. Her brothers, on the other hand...

They always made a mess of it, in a way that had her in stitches, unable to breathe from laughing so hard by the end of the day.

A wave of sadness hit her from nowhere, as Zaharra realized how much she had missed in her months away.

She had half a mind to turn and head towards the fields to see if her brothers were out there and if they needed any help bringing the vysha in for the night, but she knew she would just be procrastinating the inevitable. Instead, she stayed her course and took another deep breath, slowing to a walk as she neared the front door of her childhood home.

With a steadying breath, she reached for the doorknob to open the door.

Her brow furrowed slightly as she jiggled the handle.

The damned thing was locked.

She cocked her head before drifting around the side of the house to their backyard that doubled as the training field for her mother's students.

No one was outside.

Which was very odd, considering the time of day it was.

Zaharra turned on her heel, striding back the way she came, and gripped the front door handle in her hands.

The door didn't even budge an inch.

In all her life, she could count on one hand the number of times the front door had been locked, and every time was because her whole family had gone on vacation.

She shimmied her way to the side, small bushes under their living room window catching on her pant legs, little burs getting stuck in her laces. Cupping her hands, she plastered her face against the window.

Damn her luck.

The house was dark.

More than that, it was pristine and tidy in a way she knew her father cleaned before a huge family outing.

Relief washed over her slightly.

Looks like she didn't have to disappoint her family quite yet in her failure to get into the queen's guard.

On the other hand...

Zaharra took a step back and out of the bushes before wrinkling her nose.

When Zaharra and her eldest brother were going through a rebellious phase, and sneaking out at night, her parents had invested in magical locks to keep the house locked up tight.

There was no way she was getting into the house until her parents got back.

With a long sigh, she turned and headed towards the barn, the one with dedicated stalls for the older and pregnant vysha. It also housed all the shearing equipment, along with a small basic shower to hose off during the muddy season before coming into the house and, most importantly, a huge loft where they stored excess hay bales.

A loft she was going to be sleeping in until her family got home. Lucky for her, it was summer, and the nights were still warm enough to sleep outside.

Pushing the door to the barn open, Zaharra made a beeline straight towards the shower. Goddess only knew what she looked like after three days on the road. She tossed her travel bag to the side and stripped, turning on the cold water and stepping underneath the rough spray. She showered quickly, not a fan of the cold water even on hot days, then pulled out her last clean outfit tucked away at the bottom of her bag.

A light linen sleeveless tunic paired with her well-loved trousers that were a cross between workout leggings and loungewear. Comfortable and just tight enough to define her legs, but still breathable enough for the heat of summer.

Zaharra scowled at her boots and sweaty socks, not wanting to put those things on again for at least a million years. As much as she loved her sturdy boots, and really, any boots, her feet ached from her travels. Plus, she didn't have a spare pair of socks and refused to put on any dirty ones after finally getting all cleaned up.

She glanced around the stables quickly before spying a suspicious strap of leather sticking out from the top of a cabinet. Zaharra stretched up onto her tiptoes to grab it and a pair of old sandals she thought she had lost years ago tumbled to the ground.

"Score!" she exclaimed, a little too loudly, and a startled huff erupted from behind her.

She turned in surprise and wandered over to the stall she didn't think was occupied and peeked over.

A very pregnant vysha shook its head at her before going back to munching the hay in the stall's corner. She reached out to pet its back, checking to make sure the vysha's water bucket was full before checking on the rest of the stalls.

They were all empty and clean.

"Just you and me then, little lady," she murmured, scratching behind the vysha's ears.

Her stomach took the one second of silence to make itself heard, and Zaharra chuckled slightly.

"Well... it's just you and me *after* I get back from the tavern. I'm starving."

The Windy Tavern

Dusk was fast approaching by the time Zaharra reached the Windy Tavern. This place always held her fancy. It was farther away from the main street, on the opposite side of the town, but they also served some of the best bread along with a potato and meat dish that kept Zaharra and plenty of others coming back for more.

They also had some of the best fruit-infused mead, or so Zaharra heard. She was never one to go out on the town to drink, always having to wake up early to help on the farm and train with her mother.

Tonight, though, she wouldn't mind a drink or even two.

She had a lot on her mind and needed to figure out how to break the news to her family that she didn't get chosen to be in the queen's guard, effectively ending their family's legacy.

With those thoughts quickly dampening her mood, Zaharra stepped into the rambunctious tavern.

She scouted out the crowd, mostly orcs that lived in town, though she noticed the band playing was peculiar and clearly travelers. A group of oddly dressed humans and a bear, most definitely a shifter, playing the drums were on stage.

Snorting slightly, she narrowed her eyes. She was mistaken. There were at least a couple of elves mixed in with the humans.

Zaharra briefly wondered what had brought the strange group to the Violet Plains and where they were headed afterwards.

Her town wasn't a stranger to groups passing through, as they were on the main road towards the Midnight Mountains and to human villages beyond it.

Zaharra clapped her hands with the rest of the folks in the tavern as she made a beeline towards one of the few open booths. This one was small and near the back, far enough away from the stage to enjoy the ruckus yet still able to have a conversation with Meerek, who she spied working behind the bar. She waved, catching her attention.

Meerek waved back before making an annoyed face and clapping her hands over her ears. The bear on stage had accidentally spilled the drum set onto the ground, knocking down one elf in the process.

The elf sprang to their feet and tackled the bear, and they went rolling across the stage, upsetting the rest of the singers. Zaharra grimaced as a full brawl between the group erupted.

Four orcs wearing the Windy Tavern embroidered shirts jumped onto the stage and broke them up, hauling away the bear just as it shifted back into human form.

Zaharra slapped a hand to her mouth to stop from laughing as a cloud of fine mist shrouded the bear for an instant before dissipating and leaving a very naked human in its wake. He ran offstage and out the side door, the group following hot on his heels.

A giggle escaped Zaharra as she watched Meerek lower her hands and laugh along with everyone else in the tavern as an invisible weight on her shoulders lifted. She hadn't realized until now how much she missed simple, fun nights in her town.

While at the queen's city, she had been immersed with so many other beings around the world, from humans, shifters, elves, and even fairies, to name a few. And while she loved the bustling diversity, the nonstop action and surprises the city offered, there was just something calming about being home.

Meerek bustled over to her booth, pulling Zaharra out of her reminiscing, and placed a steaming bowl of potato and meat stew on the table in front of her. Her mouth watered instantly.

"My shift is over in ten. You want to hang after?" Meerek asked.

Zaharra nodded ecstatically; the only thing she could do after shoving a mouthful of stew in her face.

Meerek laughed and took a step away before twirling back in excitement.

"Wait! You're officially back from the queen's city! You know what this means?"

Zaharra paused, a spoonful of stew hanging between her half-opened mouth. She shook her head slightly. "Ummm... what?"

"It means congratulations are in order! You finally know what you're going to do in life, not like we all didn't know. I mean, every woman in your family has been part of the queen's guard. But it's, like, real now, you know! It's official, and we should celebrate by getting hammered."

Zaharra shoved the spoonful of stew into her mouth, hoping Meerek wouldn't catch the grimace on her face. She nodded as Meerek dashed back to the bar quickly and disappeared.

The weight of being a failure settled back on her shoulders. It wasn't just her family that she was going to disappoint, but also her town and friends.

She glanced around the tavern again as family friends and those she knew in passing waved.

Some of them yelled out congratulations, which made her want to hunch her shoulders and sink fully into the floor.

Damn, this was going to suck when everyone finally found out.

Zaharra quickly devoured her food, scraping the bottom of the bowl just as a jug of mead slammed down on the table.

She jumped slightly, glancing up at Meerek's unhappy face.

"Guess who is working until closing tonight because of a call-out?"

Relief rushed through her as she stood up and wrapped Meerek in a hug. "No worries. Honestly, I'm tired anyway."

Meerek sighed, hugging her back something fierce before stepping away and thrusting the jug of mead into her hands. "Here. My present to you. We will catch up later and have a drink together. How long until you run off to the city again?"

Zaharra forced a smile. "I'm not going to run off without saying goodbye and having an amazing girls' day with you."

A loud shout, followed by rambunctious laughter, tore Meerek's attention away, and she cursed under her breath before wrapping Zaharra in another brief hug. "I'll stop by the farm tomorrow."

Zaharra gripped the jug of mead tighter as Meerek sauntered off, waving her arms. "Hey, losers! Get some drinks and cut the racket or get on stage and turn the racket into something we can all enjoy. Just stop doing whatever shit you're doing at the moment."

Zaharra took her opportunity to escape, and once outside, she quickly popped the cork to the mead.

She really needed a fucking drink.

"Mother! It is I, your daughter, back from the queen's city. I bring disappointment." Zaharra stumbled slightly, resting heavily on the side of a building as she giggled. Her vision blurred, and she felt warm and happy on the inside.

Well, maybe not happy, but definitely no longer worried.

"No, no, no," she shushed herself. "We can think of a better way to tell Mother about us being a failure."

She pushed herself upright and did a mock bow to the empty street in front of her before pointing to nothing. "Tis I, Zaharra, and I told the queen, it was I who did not want to be there."

She giggled again and took a swig from the jug in her hand. It had grown suspiciously light, and she hiccupped before glaring down the opening of the bottle. "Hmmm... I think you and I have a problem. Where has all my mead gone?"

Snickering, she twirled on her heel, tripping slightly. Her arms pinwheeled, and what little mead was left at the bottom of the jug sloshed about. She finally righted herself and went to check on her precious mead, when her eyes caught sight of something far better.

Squatting down, she discarded the jug to the cobblestone walkway and placed both her hands on the glass window in front of her.

The most amazing set of boots she had ever seen was on display in the shopfront.

She tipped her head back to look at the sign, squinting as the letters tried to run away, as if they didn't want her to read them.

Either this was a magical shop, or she was far more drunk than she originally thought.

Zaharra was betting on the latter.

She closed one eye, and the words magically stopped moving.

"Roakheart Trading Co." She hiccupped slightly, before pressing her hands against the glass again, eyeing the boots. She pointed her finger at them. "I want you, fuzzy winter boots. With your cute little pompom laces."

"You know, they are rated for glacial temperature and are waterproof. They aren't just for looks."

The rough voice came out of nowhere, and Zaharra acted on pure instinct.

She stood quickly and spun on the balls of her feet, hands shooting out to grab whomever dared sneak up on her.

The move was second nature, a basic takedown her mother taught all her students in first-year defense classes. Her hand locked on a wrist, her other arm shooting out to turn the speaker's head as her leg swung behind their feet and she pushed.

A loud *oomph* echoed through the streets as Zaharra followed the person down, knee landing squarely on a thick, muscled chest. She tossed her head back, sending her loose hair out of her face, and locked eyes with the most handsome goliath man she had ever seen.

Roakheart Trading Co.

KAHR COULDN'T BREATHE, AND it wasn't because he was suddenly staring up at the most beautiful orc he had ever seen.

No, it was because one minute he was finally coming back from a week of travel to see someone staring at the winter boots in his shopfront, and then the next, he was on his back with a knee grinding painfully into his chest.

He tried to suck in a breath as the beautiful orc above him snarled, "Who are you, and why did you sneak up on me, Goliath?"

"Kahr." He got his name out with the little breath he still had left. "Call me Kahr. And this is my shop."

The orc's eyebrows crinkled, her frown deepening just as a hiccup escaped her. She blinked rapidly and swayed, her dark forest-green skin paling slightly.

She looked like she was about to throw up on him.

Khar winced. "If you're going to throw up, please don't do it on me."

The orc rolled her eyes and hiccupped again. "I'm not"—*Hiccup*—"going to..." She gulped and paused, glancing up to the starry sky, and took a deep breath.

She grumbled slightly under her breath before turning to look down at him again, her unbound black hair tumbling over her shoulders and shadowing her face.

"Sweetheart, if you let me up, we can go into my shop, and I can make you some tea. I have a brew that will help sober you up."

The orc narrowed her eyes, and she opened her mouth, as if she was about to say something else, but another hiccup escaped.

Kahr managed a smile as the orc shook her head and stood, releasing his arm and finally removing her knee from his sternum. He sucked in a full breath and groaned, getting to his feet.

"Sorry about that. You startled me." She brushed her hair to the side, its length sliding down her lower back.

A slight blush highlighted her high cheekbones, and Kahr felt the air rush out of his lungs once more as his eyes roamed over the beautiful orc in front of him. His gaze snagged on her luscious full lips, before making its way to her fiery amber eyes. Starlight glinted across her rich green skin, and it took all of Kahr's strength to tear his eyes away from her and reach for his shop door. The magic locks clicked, keyed to his aura, and he twisted the handle.

Luminescent fairy lights hummed to life, and he stepped to the side, motioning for the orc to come inside. He couldn't stop his gaze from dipping as she brushed past him. Her body was an enticing mix of athleticism and sculpted curves wrapped in tight leather and cloth.

Kahr shoved his hands in his pockets to keep from doing something inherently stupid.

Like touching her.

The orc stepped in before stopping in the doorway, blocking the entrance. He looked over her shoulder, just to make sure something wasn't amiss. To his eyes, everything looked fine.

"Is something wrong?" he murmured.

"No, I've just never been in here before." She shrugged slightly before wandering through the main floor of the shop, glancing around.

Kahr let her roam, letting his gaze become watchful.

The orc female was still drunk, and while he could not care less if she broke anything in the shop, he wanted to make sure she didn't accidentally hurt herself. He placed his travel pack behind the counter and sat down on the chair. The chair that had been recently vacated by one of his few hires, and the reason why he was back so soon.

And while the timing of his hire leaving had irked him earlier, he now found he didn't mind so much as he watched the woman before him pick up the pair of boots she was ogling outside his shop minutes ago.

She giggled and flicked the little pom-poms that hung at the end of the boot laces before placing them back on the shelf.

Kahr tilted his head, giving in to studying not just her beautiful orc physique, but the way she moved. If the takedown earlier hadn't already confirmed his suspicion, the way this orc moved her amazingly athletic body did.

She was a fighter, plain and simple.

Even drunk and swaying on her feet, she was confident in her own body, in her movement, and that she could hold her own against anyone and anything.

He concentrated his gaze back on her face with her full lips, expressive amber eyes, and high cheekbones.

Then she turned and smiled at him, and Kahr forgot how to breathe all over again.

She partially sauntered and swayed to him, leaning over the counter. "I always thought all trader shops were the same. But I like yours, it's... it's different."

"I didn't want to step on the toes of the other trader in town, so I tailored mine to have what his didn't."

"Makes sense. Why sell the same things and be in competition."

Kahr nodded slightly, not really hearing what she said. Instead, he was daydreaming about running his hands through this orc's long black hair.

She hiccupped and wavered on her feet slightly, snapping Kahr back to reality.

"Tea, I promised you tea. The kitchen is in the back if you want to follow."

He slipped off the chair and grabbed one of the small sample teas from the display on the counter. Leaving the choice fully up to her, he headed towards the back and immediately started washing and filling the kettle with water. Once filled, he put it on the stove and quickly stoked a fire to life.

Relief filled him as he turned to see the orc had followed him, sitting down at the small two-person kitchen table. Her elbows rested on top as she slumped slightly, holding her head in her hands.

An urge to take her into his embrace and just hold her washed over him. The intensity of the feeling had him freezing, his breath sharp and almost painful.

He balled his hands into fists, squeezing and releasing a few times before the feeling finally left, and he trusted himself not to do anything fucking stupid.

Like pulling her hands away from her face and kissing her.

Yes, that would be fucking stupid.

Considering the fact she would probably put him on his ass before he could even feel her lips on his.

And also because it would be wildly inappropriate because she was drunk, and he would never take advantage like that.

"All right, water is on," Kahr stated a bit too loudly, and the orc woman jumped slightly, raising her head from her hands.

Shit, what the hell was he thinking.

She was on the verge of passing out. She didn't need tea. She needed to get home.

"Hey," he murmured, a little softer this time, and pulled the other chair out from the kitchen table. "Do you want me to walk you home? Or to a friend's house?"

The orc grumbled under her breath before shaking her head. "I'm in no hurry to get home and sleep in the hayloft."

Kahr blinked in surprise, slightly taken aback. Why was this beautiful orc living in a hayloft?

Before he could even ask, she pulled a battered letter from her shirt pocket and shoved it in his face.

"This... this is why I'm home so early. My family isn't even here, which I guess is"—she hiccupped and shook her head—"fine. At least I get a day or so to wallow in self-pity until they get back. Then they and the town..." She hiccupped again and almost slipped from the chair.

Kahr reached out on instinct, wrapping his hand around her elbow to keep her upright.

He was slow to release her, his heart thudding rapidly just from the feel of her smooth skin on his. She didn't seem to react to him catching her, instead continuing to talk, her words slurring slightly.

"... will be so disappointed. I mean, I passed everything. I'm a damn legacy. Look... look, I passed everything and, still, I failed in the end. Why did I fail? Oh gods, everyone is going to be so disappointed in me."

Kahr's heart clenched as the orc's voice cracked at the end. He finally released his hold, making sure she was steady before taking the letter from her hand. He was curious about what was inside and whether he could make whomever made her feel like a failure to pay in a painful way.

She motioned for him to open the letter before placing her head in her palms again.

He unfolded the worn paper and quickly gazed over the contents.

Zaharra Fairstone

Kahr glanced up slightly at the beautiful orc who now had a name.

Zaharra.

It fit her, and just the sound of it in his mind made his heart sing. He desperately wanted to say it out loud, to taste the syllables on his tongue and see how she would react when he said her name for the first time. Instead, he glanced back down and continued reading.

Fullblood orc

Twenty-three years old

Damn, he had twelve years on her. She was still so young. When he was her age, he was still wandering the realm, learning who he was and what he wanted in life.

A flash of anger sizzled through his veins.

Zaharra shouldn't feel like a failure.

She still had her whole life before her.

Kahr continued reading, if only to find out the exact reason why Zaharra was so upset and how to make her happy.

A list of passes and failures next to a range of activities that spanned from knowledge, weapons, survivability, physical prowess, and critical thinking were listed on the letter.

And every one of them had a passing check until he flipped the letter over.

Below it were two sentences, and Kahr ran a finger over the smudges, most likely made by tear stains. An anger he had only felt twice in his life boiled through him at the thought of Zaharra crying.

It has been determined that though a legacy; the queen has decided you are not to be part of her guard.

Below, you can find other professions to fit your talents.

Kahr didn't even bother reading the list and fought the urge to crumple the letter and throw it into the fire on Zaharra's behalf.

The scream of the teakettle mimicked the rage inside him as he got up and moved the kettle from the fire.

"I'm sorry you..." He turned around and cut his sentence short.

She lay slumped over the table and a little snore echoed through his kitchen.

Kahr shook his head and stepped forward, scooping her into his arms before she slid off her chair.

He headed towards the spare sleeping quarters and laid her on the bed. Quickly sliding off her sandals, he placed them next to the bed before pulling the fur blanket up to her chin. She rolled to her side, burying her face in the blanket and sighed.

"Goodnight, Zaharra," Kahr whispered before pulling the door shut behind him.

Morning After

SHE WAS SLEEPING ON a cloud.

A warm, fuzzy, soft cloud that hugged every one of her curves and...

Zaharra bolted upright in alarm, clutching a fur blanket to her chest. A fur blanket she most definitely did not own.

She blinked and pushed her hair out of her face just in time for the dull ache behind her eyes to intensify.

A groan left her lips as she slammed her eyes shut and held her head in her hands.

What in the absolute gods had she done? And where was she?

Almost immediately after her thought, a blurred timeline of her drunken night played out in her mind.

Wandering around and drinking after leaving the tavern, spotting those cute boots and then a voice...

A voice that she threw on its ass, only to stare down into the most gorgeous piercing blue eyes she had ever seen. Attached to the most handsome man.

She groaned again and grabbed the fur blanket to cover her face. A face that was suddenly growing hot as her memories played out.

Zaharra lowered the blanket slightly and squinted, glancing around. There wasn't much else to see, though, besides a closet and the small bed she was in.

There wasn't even a window.

Light shone from under the closed door though, making her head ache even more, and all Zaharra wanted to do was close her eyes and fall back to sleep.

Instead, she grimaced and swung her legs forward, her bare feet hitting the cool floor. She rubbed at her head as more memories from the night before invaded her mind.

Being invited inside, for... for tea.

She remembered admiring the boots she had seen from outside. Then following the goliath to the kitchen, and then they ... talked.

Or really, she rambled, and he listened intently.

Then nothing but darkness.

"Damn it," she murmured.

She had passed out right on his table; she was sure of it. Which would explain waking up in a strange place.

He must have put her in the bed and taken off her shoes.

Which was thoughtful and kind.

But gods, what a fool she must have looked like.

She held her breath, holding back the groan that wanted to escape, as she slipped her sandals back on. What she needed to do was make a sneaky escape and forget this night had ever happened. There was a reason she never drank. She was such a lightweight and had a tendency to do embarrassing things.

Tiptoeing to the door, she pressed her ear to the wood and listened.

It was silent, and she took the opportunity to open the door and lean out.

In a split second, she registered the small sunlit kitchen and an open doorway to the left. She held her breath and tiptoed towards the open door, past a small staircase, and straight into the shopfront.

Zaharra skidded to a halt as not one, but three, patrons stared at her in surprise. Her heart thundered as the bell on the door leading outside jingled and Meerek stepped into the fucking shop.

Both their jaws dropped at the same time.

She stood frozen behind the counter, her legs refusing to work. Dear gods, could this day get any worse?

A deep and very sexy voice echoed out from her right, shaking her down to her very core. "Good morning, Zaharra. Did you sleep well?"

Her head snapped to the side, and any breath she had left disappeared as she took in the gorgeous goliath sitting behind the counter. Her eyes swept over his light grey skin, and his robust, muscular body that his plain dark tunic and light trousers did nothing to hide.

His lips quirked slightly, and he winked at her as she stared at his strong and chiseled face. He twisted his body slightly towards her, and her eyes followed his hand as he swept back his dark black shoulder-length hair from his face.

Something inside her really wanted to touch his hair, run her fingers through those silken strands and play with the adorning small bones and beads braided in. The sides of his head looked freshly shaved, and Zaharra wondered if he had to shave the sides of his head every day or if he ever let it grow out a little.

Then she wondered how it would feel if that head was between...

Her eyes grew wide as her thoughts spiraled out of control within seconds, an ache growing into full-on pulsating agony between her thighs. A hand waved between her and the goliath, breaking their eye contact, and Zaharra sucked in a strangled breath.

Meerek's confused face infiltrated her view, her hand waving frantically in front of Zaharra's eyes. "Helllllooooo? What the fuck is going on?"

She blinked and took a step back, her legs finally moving as Zaharra ran around her best friend and the other patrons of the shop. She slammed into the door, throwing herself into the bright sunlit street and sprinted all the way home.

It took Meerek about thirty minutes to find Zaharra. She was just coming out of the much-needed freezing cold shower when her friend confronted her.

"Spill the tea, now," Meerek screeched before grabbing Zaharra and hauling her out of the shower.

Zaharra clutched the towel to her body and shook her head, water flying everywhere from her sopping wet hair. "Damn it, Meerek, at least let me put my hair in a towel. I'm getting water everywhere."

"No," Meerek growled. "I need to know if you slept with the hot goliath trader, and if so, how big was it?"

"Wait, what? No, I didn't, and even if I did... I wouldn't tell... Why are you so inappropriate? Wait, do you want to sleep with him?" Zaharra stuttered, unsure of what part of Meerek's comment to focus on.

Her best friend rolled her eyes. "Any knitwhit with half a brain has wanted to sleep with that goliath ever since he bought the shop a few years ago. Kahr is alluring, at least for our town, and he's also older. You know, in that sexy, probably-knows-his-way-around-a-woman's-body type of way. Plus, he owns a business and treats his employees well, from what I've heard."

Zaharra squinted and flicked Meerek's forehead as her eyes glazed over, talking about the goliath.

Kahr.

It was a sexy name, and she was sure he had told her his name at some point last night, but her drunken brain had dumped that information.

Instead, it just kept the way his voice sounded, and his soft smile, and his face full of concern when she blabbed on and on. Telling him about...

Oh no.

She had told him how she failed and was such a disappointment. Had shoved the letter right in his face and told him to read it.

"Hey!" Meerek slapped at Zaharra's hand, which was still stretched out from flicking her. "Rude... but yes, everyone wants to sleep with him. When he's around, at least."

That drew Zaharra's attention, and Meerek continued speaking.

"He always travels, comes into town for maybe a week out of the month, tops. But he had to come back early this time because Ericka quit working for him. Did you know she had to go on bed rest because she is having twins?"

Zaharra shook her head, knowing when her friend got on a roll, there was no way she could get a word in edgewise.

Meerek waved her off with her hand. "Yes, anyways. I'm glad I'm not her. Can you imagine raising children, let alone two at once? But it is what it is, I guess. Well, she's out for a while, meaning her position running the shopfront is open. I would totally apply, but I already have too many jobs as it is. Anywho, I was passing by and saw that he was inside, and I really just wanted to take a peek at that sexy body of his." Meerek sucked in a breath and leveled her gaze to Zaharra's. "Which brings us back around to why you were sneaking out from the back rooms so early?"

Meerek turned the conversation around so easily, back onto her, and it felt like Zaharra just got whiplash.

"The night got a little weird after I drank all that mead," she murmured.

Meerek paused slightly before laughing.

Her laughter grew and grew until she doubled over.

Taking the chance to escape, Zaharra quickly got dressed, finally wrapping a towel around her hair and starting to dry it off.

"You mean to tell me you drank an entire jug of mead by yourself? You must have been so wasted." Meerek wheezed.

Zaharra shrugged. "Just a little, then I found myself outside the trader's shop staring at those cute boots."

"Oh, the ones with the fur and pompoms on the laces?"

With a sigh, Zaharra nodded, her voice cracking slightly. "Yes, the ones with the pompoms. Meerek, I need to tell you something."

"Ha! Yes, you slept with him."

"No, this is serious."

Meerek narrowed her eyes. "Like... ha-ha serious, or serious, we-should-sit-down, serious?"

Zaharra gritted her teeth. "I'm not becoming one of the queen's guards."

"You what!"

Zaharra's back straightened like a sword as her mother's scolding voice echoed through the barn.

A Disappointment

"MOM." ZAHARRA'S VOICE CRACKED.

She wasn't sure if it was out of fear or the fact she desperately needed some water after her drunken night before. Her headache that was staved off with the cold shower came roaring back, and Zaharra winced.

As her mother stormed through the barn, her father in tow, she watched as her five, no, four brothers scattered. Where was...

Oh, it didn't matter.

Her older brother was not her concern at the moment, even though his calming, analytical nature probably would have been an asset.

Zaharra's mother skidded to a halt in front of her and steadied her steely gaze at Meerek. "I think it's time you go home while I have a word with my daughter."

Meerek glanced at Zaharra, as if asking if she needed to stay.

Zaharra sucked in a deep breath. "I'll see you later. It will be fine."

Out of the corner of her eye, Zaharra watched her mother's jaw twitch.

Meerek slowly backed away and headed toward the wide-open barn doors, pausing before she stepped out to look back once more. Zaharra waved her away before turning back to face her parents.

"Speak now and explain, child," her mother gritted out between clenched teeth.

Zaharra sucked in a breath before glancing at her feet, heat blossoming across her entire face.

Shame radiated through her.

She had been so confident the day before, more than ready to explain to her parents what had happened.

But now, standing in front of them and her angry mother, she felt more like a child than a fully grown woman.

"I'm sorry, Mom," she whispered.

"That's not an explanation." Her mother's voice struck like a whip, and Zaharra flinched, hunching her shoulders.

She knew her mother would never physically strike her—even when they trained, she never did—but her words always seemed to cut straight to the bone.

"Ninie, honey." Her father's sweet, kind voice broke through the tension. "Take a breath and let her explain."

"I am trying, but our daughter is acting like a scared rabbit instead of the fighter I trained her to be."

"Zaharra, look at us."

Her father's reassuring voice relaxed her shoulders, and Zaharra glanced up ever-so-slightly. Still unable to meet her mother's terrifying gaze, she instead focused on her father's loving face.

He smiled softly. "Baby girl, just tell us what happened. I'm sure we can fix it, whatever you failed. We will make sure you pass next time."

"Because there will be a next time. I will not have my daughter, a legacy, fail at the one thing she has trained her whole life to accomplish."

Zaharra's eyes watered at her mother's words, and a single tear escaped, sliding down her face. "I passed every test. It was the queen who chose not to have me. There is no retesting."

She watched her mother's face drop, disbelief marring her stony features.

It was true; if Zaharra had failed at anything, she could have had a shot of going back and retesting, but when the queen herself decided not to have you in her guard, there was no arguing.

For the first time in her life, Zaharra watched her mother struggle for words. Watched as a myriad of emotions filtered over her mother's face until just one settled in.

Disappointment.

The look was worse than any words her mother could have said to her, and it felt like Zaharra had taken an arrow to the heart, deflating all the air she had in her lungs. Tears streamed down her face as her mother turned heel without a word and stalked out of the barn.

"It's going to be all right," her father whispered, wrapping her in a tight hug. She sobbed silently in her father's arms as he kissed the top of her head.

"You know, stall cleaning is on the chore list for your younger brothers."

Her father's voice rang out behind Zaharra as she finished raking fresh straw in the last stall. While most of the herd of vysha stayed in the fields and under outside shelters, they still had a few that needed to be stalled. The sickly, pregnant, and sometimes those who turned into pets.

Speaking of which, Zaharra reached her hand over the stall to pat the vysha she had grown up with.

Myra was one of the old ones, with a limp and half a horn, but she was affectionate and had done the family good in her twenty-three years. Born on the same day Zaharra had been. She had wandered into the barn a few hours ago, after her father had left, and nuzzled up to Zaharra, demanding to be fed.

It was a welcome distraction, as was cleaning the stalls.

Zaharra's father reached into the stall to give Myra's head a rub. "You're a good girl. Both of you are."

Zaharra shook her head, fighting back the tears that swelled in her eyes. "Figured I would get some work done before I head out. Don't know when I'll see Myra again, you know."

"Hmmm," her father hummed, still scratching at Myra's head. "And where do you think you're headed off to, so soon after getting back?"

Zaharra rested the rake against the stall and crossed her arms. She turned to face her father. "You saw the look Mom gave me. She might as well have just said it out loud. I'm a disappointment and failure to the family name. I shouldn't have even come back."

Her father shook his head once before turning to look at her. "Didn't know you had the ability to read minds, baby girl. Did you pick that up in the queen's city?"

Zaharra shook her head and went to reach for the rake again, desperate to do something, *anything.* "You know I'm right."

"If you say so, but when has your mother ever not said what she was thinking out loud. If she truly thought that, she would have said it. But I didn't come in here to talk about that."

"Then why did you come in here?" Zaharra pushed at the freshly raked hay, moving it about.

"To see how my only daughter is doing? To see if she is ever going to make it back into the house, or do you plan on sleeping in the barn all summer?"

Zaharra shrugged. "I don't know if I can face Mother and that look again. I don't want to leave, but it might be for the best."

"How about you and I make an agreement?"

"What type of agreement?"

"It's summer. You will do perfectly well sleeping in the loft here in the barn. You and your mother can have some space to think, while I can have my favorite child not homeless and living on the streets."

Zaharra snorted and tried to hide the smile forming on her lips. "I'm your favorite?"

Her father bumped her with his shoulder and smiled. "Of course you are. You're my baby girl. And you have never disappointed me a day in your life, and you never will."

Zaharra leaned in and wrapped her arms around her father's sturdy shoulders. "Thank you, Papa."

Her father chuckled, squeezing her back. "You know your mother isn't the best at communicating her feelings. But believe me, she loves you. It's just a shock. We weren't expecting you to be home, and to have *that* news... And after we just got back from dropping your brother off. It pushed her over the edge."

Zaharra pushed back ever-so-slightly, her brow crinkling. "Wait, where... what were you doing?"

"We dropped Dalin off at the port. He's doing the second half of his political advisor journeyship."

"Oh," Zaharra said softly. "I guess I won't be seeing him again... For how long is he gone this time?"

Her father's gaze softened. "About a year."

Zaharra gritted her jaw and nodded as a new wave of sadness tried to consume her. Dalin would have told her that there was no need to be sad before pushing his glasses up his nose and spouting off some philosophical something or another to cheer her up.

"About a year." She parroted her father's words.

He patted her on the back. "There is no need to worry about your older brother. What we need to worry about now is getting you a job. Something to get you out of this barn and your mind on newer and better things."

And just like that, the reality that she was now living in her parents' barn for the summer, and had failed at the very thing she trained her entire life for, came rushing back. Sadness and shame tried to wiggle their way back into her mind as her father started listing off a few close family friends in town she could work for.

But she didn't want to go through this whole song and dance again. Having to explain why she was back, why she would not be part of the queen's guard and deal with the pitied looks from her parents' friends.

If only there was...

Suddenly, she remembered what Meerek had said earlier.

"I have a job," she whispered.

Goddess above, what was she doing?

Lying to her father, all because of what...? She couldn't handle the pitied looks her parents' friends would give her if she worked for them?

Her father went silent, and Zaharra held her breath.

"You have a job... already?" He squinted at her.

"Yes, at the trader ... the trader's shop. You know the one with"—she motioned with her hand—"the boots."

"Boots?"

"Goliath. Kahr, the goliath, owns the place, and I was there yesterday, admiring the boots in the window display. You know how I like boots. Well, he's in need... He needs a full-time helper. So I have a job already."

Oh goddess, now she had to go back to Kahr's shop and beg the hot goliath for a job.

Or maybe she could just pretend she had a job there and just disappear for a few days a week.

Which might work if her father actually believed her. Which, from the look on his face, was a big, fat no.

Her father took a step back and frowned before shaking his head.

"All right then, you have a job already. Let's go visit this employer of yours. I want to make sure I know exactly where my baby girl is working."

Shit.

And the day just kept getting worse and worse.

Unexpected Encounter

THE LAST PERSON KAHR expected to see again today was *her*.

Yet here she was.

In his shop and with an older orc in tow.

A feather of jealousy brushed across his mind before Kahr pushed the emotion aside.

The older orc broke away, inspecting the shelves full of jars and spices, though his eyes were taking in much more than what was for sale in his shop.

Kahr focused back on the customer before him, handing them their change. When he looked back up, Zaharra was staring right at him.

Their eyes met, and she mouthed something that looked like, *Just go with it.*

His eyebrows crinkled in confusion as the older orc approached, Zaharra a few steps behind him.

"So," the older orc murmured, "this is where my daughter is working."

Kahr's confusion spread tenfold through his mind. What was this orc going on about?

He glanced over the orc's shoulder towards Zaharra, who was mouthing, *me,* making a few gestures he really couldn't figure out. Was she fishing? Climbing something? What...

The older orc glanced over his shoulder at Zaharra, who immediately clasped her hands behind her back and gave them both a smile that looked more like a grimace.

Kahr smothered a laugh, choking slightly before standing and reaching out his arm in the traditional orcish greeting. "I take it you are Zaharra's father. Sorry, it took me a second to realize. It's been an... interesting day so far."

Zaharra's father clasped his forearm in his hand, and Kahr did the same.

"And when exactly did you hire my daughter?"

They broke away, and Kahr caught Zaharra trying to mouth something. He shook his head and smiled. "Yesterday, when she got back into town. She is a real go-getter, your daughter. Marched right into my shop and demanded a job. And how could I refuse?"

Zaharra's father harrumphed, glancing back at her.

Kahr took the opportunity to mouth back to her while her father's back was turned away from him, *Do you really want a job?*

She nodded. "Yes. See, I told you I had a job. And it starts..."

"Tomorrow morning," Kahr butted in, helping her out.

Zaharra's father glanced between the two of them and nodded. "All right. All right." A slow smile overtook his face as he stroked his jaw. "I like this. This is good. I approve."

Kahr furrowed his brow, not sure what the orc was referring to, but from the look on Zaharra's face, it seems she was just as confused.

"Okay, Papa. We should... go. Yes, we should go." Zaharra grabbed her father's arm, and all but dragged him towards the door. She glanced over her shoulder, giving Kahr a look he could only describe as bewildered.

He lifted his hand and waved. "See you tomorrow. Bright and early."

Kahr groaned into his pillow, knowing full well he would not get anymore sleep. It was still hours until he had to open his shop, but it didn't matter. He had barely slept anyway, so he might as well get his ass out of bed.

He rolled over to stare at the ceiling.

Fuck, what in the gods' names had he been thinking giving Zaharra a job.

He had intended to go find her yesterday evening after closing. He couldn't get her out of his mind. She was just so much... of everything.

Everything Kahr looked for in a woman.

Funny, strong, beautiful.

Inside and out.

He had plans to court her, to learn more about her.

And now...

Now he was her employer.

Kahr knew better than to entertain a relationship between boss and employee.

It would become a complicated mess if they wound up in a relationship and then it ended. Plus, he didn't want to put Zaharra in any type of situation that questioned their power dynamic.

He wanted her to say yes, not because he was her boss, but because she actually wanted to.

Though knowing what little he already knew about her, Zaharra would probably beat him up before doing anything she didn't want to do.

But it didn't matter, though.

He refused to even put himself or Zaharra in that type of situation.

He scrubbed at his face and sat up.

Kahr had done this to himself, and now he was going to deal with the consequences.

And he would keep his hands and mouth and all the things he wanted to ...

Fuck, no.

Best stop that type of thinking right here and now.

So long as Zaharra was working for him, Kahr would treat her as he would any other employee.

And he would stop having inappropriate thoughts about the things he really wanted to do with her.

With a growl, he threw himself out of bed, stomping out the door and across the hall to the bathroom.

He slammed the door harder than he needed to and yanked the knob in the shower to the coldest setting.

Kahr stepped in and leaned his forehead against the tiled wall, his inhale sharp as ice-cold water drenched his body.

Deep inside, he knew this would not be the last time he took a painfully cold shower.

The First Day

Zaharra honestly didn't know what she was doing.

She had slept like crap, tossing and turning until she finally gave up on sleep and instead tried to silence her mind in the only way she knew.

After an hour of slow katas, followed by a moonlit run, she ended with a much-needed cold shower to cool her equally overheated skin and mind. Then she dressed and headed out.

She was early, embarrassingly so, when she reached Roakheart Trading Co. As she stood outside the shopfront door, the inside still as dark as it was outside, she contemplated her next move.

It had been nice of Kahr to cover for her. She had even seen a hint of a smile, a glint in his eye when he just went along with her lie.

And while Zaharra really wanted to get to know Kahr, she also knew she had overstepped and put him in an awkward position.

It wasn't like her to take advantage.

No, she decided.

She would ask for the job properly and give Kahr an out.

Though, knowing her father, he would probably stop by just to see her at work...

"Uhggg, how did I get myself into such a mess?" Zaharra sighed and rubbed at her face.

Oh, she knew exactly how she got into this mess. She did not know what to do with her life now that she would not be in the queen's guard and that news had broken her brain.

And apparently a broken brain meant becoming a lying liar face who was also a coward who couldn't deal with a few pitied looks from family friends.

No, she had to fix this now.

She would thank Kahr for covering for her, then go home and tell her father she didn't actually have a job at the traders' shop.

Then she would...

Soft fae lanterns flickered, illuminating inside of the shop, and on pure instinct, Zaharra dropped to a crouch. She scuttled slightly to the left, to the window with the most displays, and lifted her head slightly.

Her eyes widened, her breath hitching as she watched Kahr walk through the doorway separating the shop from the backrooms. His fingers danced over the buttons of his long-sleeve shirt, hiding his magnificent chest from the world. He reached behind the counter, bending just so the shirt rode up slightly on his side, revealing muscles that made Zaharra bite her bottom lip.

Kahr righted himself, and Zaharra's jaw went slack as she watched his back and shoulder muscles bunch under his shirt. He put a skinny book on the counter that also held the register, and as he lifted his head, his piercing blue eyes met her gaze.

"Fuck," Zaharra whispered as she realized Kahr could clearly see her. Panic sliced through her veins, her cheeks already warming from embarrassment as Kahr strode across the shop to the front door.

She stood quickly as the little bell announcing the door opening jingled and sucked in a deep breath.

"I was just—"

"You're here—"

They both spoke, cutting each other off.

Zaharra bit her lip as Kahr shook his head.

"Sorry. You were saying?"

His deep voice curled over her in a way that felt way too intimate.

Kahr had a voice that was made to whisper dirty, dirty things in the dark.

"Of course, I'm here," Zaharra whispered, her voice going husky. "Where else would I be?"

Kahr opened his mouth before snapping it shut and clearing his throat. "I... I was... you. You are here early. That was what I was going to say."

His words snapped Zaharra back to reality. "Yes, yes. Sorry. I, ah, I actually came by to say thank you. Yesterday must have been really weird for you, and you didn't need to cover for me the way you did, and that..."

She trailed off as Kahr ran his hand through his hair, his lips pulling into a soft smile.

"Happy to help. Did you want to come in?"

Zaharra nodded and hurried inside, careful not to graze any part of her body against Kahr's as she passed by. She really didn't trust herself, unsure of what she would do if her body reacted any more to Kahr than it was at the moment. She had to focus, stay on task. She had a plan, and she was going to execute it.

She stepped to the side as Kahr walked past, close enough for her to catch a whiff of sandalwood and sweet spice. Her heartbeat seemed to fill the silence as she dropped her gaze. Even in the movable, loose-fitting trousers Kahr wore, she could make out the outlines of a nice ass and thick thighs.

Zaharra squeezed her hands into tight fists and wrenched her eyes up. Kahr stood behind the counter, blocking his body from her view, and internally she let out a sigh of relief.

She really needed to concentrate.

"You don't have to give me a job," she blurted out.

Kahr cocked an eyebrow, looking like he was about to say something, but Zaharra barreled over him. "What I mean is, thank you for going along with yesterday, but you have no obligation to give me a job, and I don't even know why I told my father I had one, here of all places. I mean, I... I need a job, and I really don't know what I'm doing with my life, but..." She sucked in a breath and started pacing, her mind going a mile a minute. "But a job, any job, would get my mind off the fact that I don't know what to do now that—"

"Zaharra."

Kahr's voice infiltrated her growing anxiety, and she glanced up to see he was standing in front of her.

She lifted her chin to look at Kahr's handsome face and bottled up the urge to do something stupid like reach out and caress his slate-grey skin. Damn, how did she just now realize he was a good half a foot taller than her? It was oddly sexy.

"I'm hiring help. The job is yours if you want it, along with the spare room downstairs."

Oh no, that was way too tempting.

She felt herself nod.

"Is that a yes?"

"Yes, yes to the job. The spare room is a kind gesture but not needed." She heard herself answer, but it felt like an out-of-body experience.

Kahr's eyes roamed her face before he nodded. "Well, the offer still stands. Even if it is just for a night here or there. I remember you saying last night you were sleeping in a hayloft."

She couldn't help staring at his lips while he spoke and was barely listening.

"And as far as being a disappointment..."

Wait, what was he saying?

Zaharra shifted her gaze and concentrated on his words.

"Take it from one disappointment to another. When I was your age, I was still figuring out who I was and what I wanted to do in life." He motioned to the surrounding shop. "And I turned out okay."

Zaharra stared at him, the silence stretching between them until the color of Kahr's cheekbones darkened slightly and he reached up to rub at his chin. "Or at least I think I did... I am... I was just... I..."

"Meerek mentioned you were older."

Oh gods, why did she just blurt those words out?

"What?"

"What?" she fired back at him, a little more high-pitched than she needed to and her heart began racing.

What was happening to her? Why was she acting like this?

Kahr smirked. "You were talking about me with your friends?"

Zaharra's jaw dropped, unsure of what she was about to say as the jingle of the front door saved her from embarrassing herself any more in their disastrous conversation.

She stepped to the side as an older orcish woman hobbled in, leaning heavily on her cane.

She narrowed her eyes at the two of them before focusing on Zaharra.

"You work here?"

Zaharra nodded. "Yes, ma'am."

The woman nodded. "Good. I need your help with my shopping."

Lunchtime Bet

HE WAS AN IDIOT.

Kahr had told himself those four words repeatedly for the last three and a half hours. The hours in which his shop opened were some of the busiest, teetering off during midday and then busy again right before dusk. Right now, they were falling into the steady decline right before a lull and he did not know what to say to Zaharra when there wasn't the distraction of people around.

She took to the shop and its customers like a natural, eager to help, actively listening, and giving everyone the attention they deserved. When she couldn't find something or the customers needed something to be special ordered, she glanced at Kahr, and every time her expressive amber eyes met his, he swore his heart leapt from his chest.

Hence why he was an idiot.

He told himself this morning to treat her like any of his current and past employees, but he knew deep down he would do anything for her if she just asked.

He hadn't fallen for someone this hard, this quick, since he was a damn teenager.

Kahr rang up the customer in front of him and kept his eyes down, concentrating on the accounts and special-order ledgers in front of him.

He needed to put in some orders soon and...

His heart raced as the scent of honeysuckles and wild oranges infiltrated his space, his body knowing who was approaching before he even looked up.

Zaharra leaned on the counter, pushing a strand of hair out of her face and behind her ear. Her loose braid had come undone in the last hour or so, and she hadn't bothered redoing it.

Kahr's hands itched, and it took all his willpower not to reach out and run his fingers through her silky black strands. He wanted to know if her intoxicating scent came from her hair or her skin.

Instead, he cleared his throat and lifted his eyes to meet hers.

A low, rumbling growl echoed through his shop, and Zaharra's eyes grew wide as she slapped a hand on her stomach.

Kahr chuckled as his stomach answered hers.

She pointed at him, a wide smile overtaking her face. "Yes, what he said."

Kahr snorted and shook his head, shutting the ledger book. "I think that is our cue for lunch. I have leftovers along with fresh bread and cheese in the cold storage, if you want to join me. Or you are more than welcome to head out and come back after."

Zaharra bit her lip, and Kahr stifled a groan. His grip tightened on the ledger, so much so he wouldn't be surprised if it would have his fingertips permanently etched into the leather cover.

"I wouldn't mind having lunch with you."

The soft tone of her voice made Kahr unclench his hand and, apparently, his jaw too. He hadn't realized his whole body tensed up while waiting for her answer.

"All right, off to the kitchen, then." He turned and was halfway down the short hall before he realized Zaharra wasn't following. He glanced over his shoulder and caught her hesitating, glancing at the door. "This is the slowest part of the day. The bell will announce if any customers come in, but I bet you anything, there won't be anyone for the next few hours."

Zaharra snorted, a smirk overtaking her lips, and if mischief were an expression, Kahr swore she wore it right now. She cocked an eyebrow. "Anything. You would bet anything?"

He choked out a laugh. "You want to bet?"

She all but sauntered up to and past him, flipping her hair over her shoulder. "Ya, it will be fun. We can figure out what to bet while you make me food."

"I mean, you said you would bet anything... I don't see why a magical spear of destiny is so out of the realm of possibilities."

Kahr rolled his eyes at Zaharra's words and bit into his sandwich. He shook his head and swallowed. "One," he stated and pointed at her. "You could barely say that with a straight face."

Zaharra smiled and took another bite of the sandwich he had made her out of leftover chicken breast, fresh cheese, and a cranberry sauce he had made himself.

"And second," he continued, "magical spear of destiny... something like that doesn't exist. Might as well ask for a genie in a bottle and three wishes while you're at it."

"That," she said with a full mouth. "I want a genie in a bottle, and I'll wish for a magical spear of destiny."

"And I'll wish for you to have some manners," he joked and offered her a cloth napkin. She took it with a glare before wiping her mouth and the bit of sauce off her chin.

"That would be a wish wasted. I have impeccable manners."

Kahr leveled a stare at Zaharra that made her giggle. A giggle that went straight to his heart. Fuck, he was in over his head already.

"Says the woman who put me on my ass the first time I spoke to her, and then rushed out of my shop the next day without so much as a thank you for letting her drunk ass stay in my guest bed. Then, on that same day, demanded a job from me. After, of course, gossiping to her friends about me and my old age, apparently. Though I wouldn't say thirty-five is old."

Zaharra coughed and finished chewing, all while shaking her head. "First off, no, it actually isn't. Second, Meerek and I weren't gossiping. She just talks and I listen. Third, thank you for letting my drunk ass sleep in your guest bed. And last but not least, you shouldn't have startled me, and I wouldn't have put you on your ass. Though, you should really work on that."

Kahr choked on his sandwich slightly and took a long gulp of water. He definitely didn't hear her right. "I should... work on my ass?"

"What? No." Zaharra shook her head frantically, and Kahr grinned as a blush overtook her cheeks. She motioned at him. "You should learn some basic countermoves. The takedown I did was really, really basic. A child could do it."

Kahr nodded. "Well... let that be our bet, then. If a single customer doesn't come in for the next hour, you teach me how to defend myself from that takedown."

Gods, he really wanted her to touch him, even if it meant she was throwing him on the ground over and over again.

She seemed to mull it over. "All right, I can do that... if you win. But we still need to figure out what I win if a customer does come in."

Kahr scratched at his chin before leaning back in his chair. "Could I interest you in a pair of boots?"

Zaharra burst out laughing. "Really, out of everything and anything, we are betting a pair of boots and getting taught a super basic self-defense move?"

Kahr reached out his hand. "Yes. Want to shake on it?"

She reached out, grasping his forearm, and he curled his fingers around hers. Her skin was warm and soft under his fingers and, fuck, he really just wanted to pull her into his lap and bet on something else.

Something he really shouldn't be thinking about as Zaharra's boss.

Her eyes met his, and he swore, just for a moment, she wanted the same.

The jingle of the bell broke the moment, and they both released their hands at the same time.

"Looks like you just won a pair of boots," he whispered.

A Run to Outrun the Mind

ZAHARRA STARED UP AT the rafters in the barn, her eyes slightly blurry from just waking up. She had been having the best fucking dream ever, involving her sexy boss and his bed. And she had woken up right in the middle of it.

She groaned and rolled over, her hands itching to finish what her dream had started.

These past two weeks working at the shop with her incredibly sexy boss had tested all her patience. The way he looked at her made Zaharra think he felt the same way, but Kahr never made a move.

She tried her best at flirting, but she had never been good at that type of thing.

Zaharra sighed again, this time shoving her face into her pillow. Between all her training to become part of the queen's guard and chores around the family farm, she never had time for dating.

To be fair, she hadn't even been that curious about it either. It was only after prompting from Meerek that she pursued one boy, but after a month, she ended it. She just never felt that... spark.

That was, until she saw Kahr for the first time.

Zaharra grumbled and shoved her face harder into her pillow.

What was she thinking?

Obviously, her feelings were one-sided, or else he would have said something already.

Which meant she had to just deal with how hot, kind, patient, and funny her boss was. And she really had to stop fantasizing about him touching her.

And fantasizing about him when she touched herself.

"Yup, I'm going for a run. That's what I'm going to do," she grumbled to herself and sat up.

She wasn't sure what time it was, only that the darkness was still a stain across the sky when she finally emerged from the barn dressed in a tight, sleeveless top and equally tight but stretchy pants. She leaned down to check the laces on her beat-up boots were double knotted.

Zaharra had considered wearing the new boots she had won with that silly bet with Kahr.

A flirting failure on her part.

She had even tried sauntering in front of him.

Yet again, another fail.

But the boots reminded Zaharra of Kahr and this run was supposed to get her out of her head to stop thinking about her boss.

She took off at a fast sprint, trying to outrun her own mind. Running always helped with that, and she had a lot to outrun.

She concentrated on her breathing and the sound of her feet hitting the hard-packed ground as her stride evened out. Turning on instinct, she headed left, then right. Take another left and left and ...

"Shit," Zaharra breathed out and sped up, sprinting past the trader's shop and her hopefully sleeping boss she couldn't stop thinking about.

"What the fuck is wrong with me?" she growled and continued running, turning this way and that, desperately trying to empty her mind.

She finally reached the edge of town and turned off the main road to a smaller path as dawn crested, darkness turning to light grey before the sun peaked out.

Zaharra wasn't sure where she was going, only that her feet kept her moving forward. Her mind had finally quieted—at least about Kahr.

After a few miles, she stopped under the shadow of a huge tree. Her chest heaved, and she stretched her arms up, hands to her head as she stared out across the dancing fields of violet flowers. The wind was cool against her cheeks, and she closed her eyes, lifting her face towards the rising sun.

It was peaceful, at least for a few moments, before her thoughts caught up with her.

With a sigh, she opened her eyes.

Great, she got less than one minute of peace before her mind started spiraling again, this time about what she was supposed to do with the rest of her life.

She would rather think about her sexy boss and his gorgeous smile. The way the corners of his eyes crinkled when he laughed or how when he concentrated on the ledger and books, his mouth slightly down-turned and brow furrowed in concentration.

She shook her head and turned, only to stop again. Her breath hitched slightly as her gaze caught sight of thick, dark clouds in the distance. The wind changed directions, blowing harder, and Zaharra cursed under her breath.

They were in peak summer season, and summer in the Violet Plains brought violent windstorms. With how fast that cloud was moving and building in on itself, Zaharra knew it was going to hit the town soon.

And she didn't want to be out in the open when it did.

"Shit, shit, shit," she growled as she took off at a sprint back into town.

Bells for the storm were already ringing as her long legs ate up the distance, the blue sky turning grey, as if the day had already passed her by. She slowed, skidding to a halt as she passed the back of the shop.

What in the...

"What are you doing?"

Her boss glanced up at her, startled blue eyes meeting hers as he lifted two fifty-pound rice sacks onto his shoulders.

She couldn't help but notice how his muscles flexed in the sleeveless shirt he wore, or how his gaze suddenly shifted to her body, if only for a moment, before coming back to her face.

"There is a storm coming," Kahr grunted.

"No shit. Why are you outside? Wait, wasn't this shipment supposed to come in tomorrow?"

Zaharra was already moving, grabbing a medium-sized crate from the cart, filled with gods only knew what.

"Yes, well, surprise, it got here early. The driver already found shelter with his vysha at the local inn. I wanted to get as much product inside as possible before the storm comes through the town."

Zaharra pushed her way past Kahr and stacked the crate to the side into the storage room. He followed and unceremoniously threw the burlap sacks of rice into the corner. "You should head home before the storm hits."

She shook her head and pushed past, her arm brushing over his. A shiver ran down her spine at the touch, but she kept moving, leaning over the cart to grab another crate.

Zaharra glanced over her shoulder, swearing she heard a groan, but it must have been the wind, which had picked up exponentially. She handed off the crate to Kahr, who was standing in the doorway. "I'm staying to help."

He sighed, glancing up at the sky just as the clouds above opened up, warm rain coming down in sheets.

"Fine. But we need to hurry."

Confession

KAHR COULDN'T STOP LOOKING at Zaharra every time she turned to offload more product from the cart. The rain drenched them both from head to toe, making her already tight clothes tighter, and Kahr was having trouble breathing.

He really needed to get his mind out of his pants and concentrate on getting his shop locked down for the storm, the wind already making them sway on their feet.

As he grabbed the last crate from the cart, he stepped inside, Zaharra following close behind. She struggled with the door and Kahr dropped the crate in his hands to the floor before coming up behind her. His chest pressed against her back as he grasped the wooden door bar with her. With both of them pulling, the door finally shut, and Zaharra leaned over slightly to throw the latch.

Kahr took a hasty step back, knowing all too well if he hadn't, his hands would have done something extremely inappropriate. The howling wind filled the silence as Zaharra turned around, scrunching her nose slightly as she grabbed her mess of hair and flung it behind her shoulder. The wet slap against her back jarred Kahr back into reality.

"Come on." He turned on his heel. "Let's get you out of those wet clothes before you catch a cold."

His eyes widened at what he just said, but he kept walking, hoping Zaharra wouldn't find any other meaning in it. He gripped the banister on the stairs leading upstairs a little too tightly, his body all too aware of who followed so close behind him.

Then the stairs abruptly ended, and Kahr cursed internally.

Why were there so little steps between the first and second story of his shop?

He opened the door to his bedroom and went to the standing wardrobe, pulling out one of his favorite long sleeve tunics and a pair of lounging pants. Turning on his heel, he held them out to Zaharra. "Bathroom is right outside, opposite side of the stairs. If you wanted to get cleaned up."

Her smile made his heart beat a mile a minute as she took the clothes from his hands. Her fingers brushing against his made Kahr's pants tighten, and he prayed to all the gods and goddess's he could think of that she wouldn't glance down.

You are her boss; he screamed in his head as his body all but betrayed how Kahr really felt towards Zaharra.

The god of luck was apparently on his side today, though, as she turned without looking down, and hurried off to the bathroom. As the door closed behind her, Kahr felt his knees weaken, and he slumped against his bed, gripping the post for stability.

Fuck. Fuck. Fuck.

He was so fucking screwed.

He wasn't sure how much longer he could keep this up.

Just the thought of Zaharra getting naked in his bathroom was throwing his mind into a loop, and only after a crack echoed did Kahr realize he just broke his own bedpost.

Shaking out his hand, he hurriedly changed and dried his hair out before all but running down the staircase to the kitchen. He fired up the stove, busying his hands to do something, really anything, to keep himself distracted. He definitely wasn't thinking about Zaharra and the way her clothes had been so tight against her body. Or the way her body had moved while helping him race against the clock, unloading the shop merchandise before the storm hit.

He definitely wasn't picturing the way her clothes seemed to melt even tighter against her body as the rain poured around them.

"Just think about something else," Kahr growled as his mind kept betraying him, once again bringing his beautiful employee to the forefront of his mind.

"What was that?" Zaharra's voice rang out behind him, and Kahr sucked in a startled breath before turning to glance over his shoulder.

Shit. Fuck. Shit.

He was an idiot.

Why had he given her his clothes?

How was seeing her dressed in his favorite tunic and lounge pants going to help him keep his hands to himself?

He owned a damn shop, for fuck's sake.

He sold clothing.

And yet she hadn't said a word against his blunder. As if....

No, he really couldn't let himself start thinking like that.

Zaharra was just being nice.

She wasn't being flirty with him this past week. The way she had looked at him upstairs hadn't been with longing, and he had to stop thinking about her this way. He had to stop thinking into every single look she sent his way. Stop dissecting every little thing she said to him.

He glanced back at the stove, pulling the now whistling kettle off the burner and began making tea. "I hope you don't mind. I figured some tea would be nice while we wait out the storm. I could also scrounge up something to eat if you would like?"

Zaharra sat at the kitchen table and nodded. "I would love something to eat. I'm famished. Also, tea is a great idea."

Kahr placed the teapot on the table with a couple of mugs and then turned back around to look through his cold storage. "If you don't mind me asking, why were you out so early this morning?"

He pulled out a half basket of eggs and a whole package of maple-infused ham slices. He had gotten them yesterday from the butcher, and the eggs a few days ago. Turning, he held them up. "What do you think? Ham, eggs. Still have some leftover bread I can toast up."

Zaharra pursed her lips against the mug she held and nodded. There was a far-off look in her eyes that he really didn't like, but Kahr knew if she wanted to talk about what was on her mind, she would.

"I was out for a run," she finally said and sipped at her tea.

Kahr resisted the urge to glance over his shoulder, instead concentrating on frying up the eggs and ham slices in a skillet.

"I really couldn't sleep. Too much... going on in my mind. Running has a tendency to clear my head."

"Did it work?" Kahr asked as he flipped the ham slices and moved the eggs out of the pan. He reached for the bread and sliced a few pieces before putting them in the skillet.

The wind slammed against the window shutters, howling around the shop as silence stretched between them.

Kahr was about to tell Zaharra he was sorry for being noisy, and she didn't need to answer his question, when she finally started speaking again.

"For a brief moment, then I saw the storm moving in and sprinted back into town."

"Ah." Kahr chuckled and flipped the ham and bread. "So you didn't just come sprinting to work, hoping to beat the storm?"

Zaharra chuckled right back. "Yes, that is what I thought. I thought, oh no, a huge violet windstorm I'm terrified of is about to hit the town. Let's go to work."

Kahr moved the cooked ham to the plate with the eggs, along with the toast, and turned off the stove. Setting the plate of food in the middle of the kitchen table along with some butter, he finally looked at the orc woman in front of him, her fingers tight around her mug, her face and shoulders tense.

"Why are you terrified of windstorms? Or is it all storms you have a dislike for?"

Zaharra sighed and put down her tea, before snagging a piece of bread and layering a slice of ham and an egg on top. She buttered another piece of toast and placed that one on top, making herself a sandwich. "When I was younger, maybe five or so, my older brother and I got caught in one while in the fields. We didn't hear the sirens and continued playing. We almost died that day. I've been terrified ever since of summer storms. Can't seem to get over it."

Kahr stayed silent, making his own sandwich as he sat down at the table with Zaharra. Only after he took his first bite did he speak. "I'm terrified of losing the people I care about while I'm helpless to help."

Zaharra coughed slightly, as if startled by his confession. In all their time working together this past week, they hadn't actually shared more than fun small talk. When she said nothing, Kahr continued. "I almost lost my little sister when the frozen lake we were walking on broke. I wasn't even supposed to be out that far and, of course, she followed. Didn't even notice until I heard her scream. She didn't know how to swim. I think that was the day I realized how easy it could be to lose someone you cared about. Luckily, that didn't happen, and that summer, I taught her how to swim. I was ten, and she was five."

A Moment Broken

ZAHARRA'S HEART CONTINUED TO hammer as the wind howled outside. She had told no one before how terrified she was of windstorms. Only her older brother knew the extent of her terror. And as Kahr told his story about him and his sister, Zaharra realized how much she still didn't know about her boss. In the past week they had worked together, most of what they talked about was in the present, just little things that barcly scratched the surface. She really wanted to know more about Kahr's past.

She finished her breakfast sandwich and took a swig of her now cold tea. "I didn't know you had a sister. Do you have any other siblings?"

He shook his head. "No, our mother left a few years after Noreena was born. That's my sister's name, Noreena. But our father never took another to marry. Our mother leaving turned him into a different person, and it was really just me and my sister looking out for each other growing up."

Zaharra's jaw went slack, unsure of what to say.

She could never imagine her parents separating, let alone not having them care for her or her brothers. Even with the silent treatment going on between her mother and her now, Zaharra knew if push came to shove, she could go to her mother for help.

Kahr chuckled slightly, as if embarrassed. "I'm sorry. The conversation got a little... intense."

She shook her head, her hands itching to reach out and touch Kahr's.

Instead, she curled her hands tighter around her mug to keep herself under control.

"No, I enjoy listening to you. It helps keep my mind off the storm."

Kahr cracked a smile that lit up his face, and Zaharra suppressed the urge to trace his smile lines with her fingertip.

"Well then, let's see what else..." He laughed suddenly and shook his head, leaning in across the table. Zaharra felt herself leaning closer too, being drawn in like a moth to a flame. "When Noreena was ten, she spent the whole summer convinced... Wait, do you know what mountain lymer's are? The rodents with fluffy tails, white and cream colored during the winter and tan in the summer?"

Zaharra nodded. "Yup, they are, like, five pounds, right, and run in little packs, live in burrows?"

Kahr nodded, his smile growing wider. "So one summer, I convinced my sister that they could talk."

Zaharra snorted with laughter, and Kahr chuckled alongside her.

"We were out checking traps, and Noreena was being particularly annoying that day. She was dragging her feet, and I got pretty far ahead. I was resetting a trap behind this big tree when, suddenly, I hear Noreena gasp so loud. I glance around the tree and then I see it. She is in a standoff with this big, fat lymer and they are just staring at each other. She wasn't in any danger, so I wasn't really worried, and then, to my surprise, she crouches down and tries to talk to it."

Zaharra shook her head, her smile growing wide as she imagined the scene playing out right before her.

"Neither of them has a clue I am behind the tree, so of course, I get this idea, and I made my voice as high pitched and squeaky as I could and just start talking, pretending I was the lymer."

"Oh gods." Zaharra laughed, her hands reaching out to grab Kahr's. "Please tell me you remembered what you said?"

Kahr sucked in a deep breath. "'My name is Timru and I am lymer royalty! You dare look upon me without bowing. Off with your head.'"

Zaharra's whole body shook, her laughter turning silent, barely able to breathe as Kahr continued, his thumb sliding back and forth on her hand in a comforting motion.

"And of course, the lymer runs away after that, and I come out from behind the tree, asking what is going on, and she spends the whole walk back to the camp trying to convince me that the lymer spoke to her. After that, she refused to trap them, refused to even eat them until Father made me tell her it was me the whole time."

Zaharra couldn't help it as she leaned forward even more, the pull towards Kahr almost magical. His gaze softened, dropping to her lips, his hand still in hers, and Zaharra felt her stomach flutter.

They both jumped as the weather sirens wailed, breaking the moment to let the town know the storm was over.

Kahr's hand slipped from hers as he pulled away, and Zaharra's chest tightened as a feeling she had never experienced before washed over her in that moment.

A wanting need, a burning desire that pulsated through her whole body.

She had never wanted like this before.

Zaharra gulped, her throat going dry as she straightened, and Kahr cleared his throat. He avoided looking at her, instead sliding out from his chair and walking to the small window to look outside.

"It looks all clear. Not a cloud in sight." Kahr's rough voice echoed, strangely lower than usual.

"Kahr..." Zaharra whispered.

"You should get going. I'm sure your family is wondering where you are. Plus, it's your day off. Though I will pay you for the few hours this morning. For helping me get all the merchandise in before the storm hit."

Zaharra's whole body tensed, going hot and cold at the same time.

She felt her eyes burn, her chest aching. Her chair squeaked, loud in the now silent kitchen as her feet hit the floor.

"You don't need to pay me for helping you," she croaked out, her throat thick from holding back the tears in her eyes.

Kahr shook his head, still looking out the window. "Of course I'm going to pay you. You are my employee. Now you should enjoy your day off. And you don't need to come in so early tomorrow."

Zaharra sucked in a breath, taking in how tense Kahr's whole body was. Clearly, he wanted her gone, and she wasn't about to beg him to look at her. If anything, this dismissal showed her that the moment they had just shared was a mistake.

Nothing more than her boss trying to be nice and distract her from the storm.

"I guess I'll see you tomorrow, then," Zaharra whispered and turned away, stalking towards the back entrance of the shop.

Wiping at the single tear that rolled down her cheek, she tried to pretend that her heart wasn't breaking.

Fuck, she was in love with her boss, and he wanted nothing to do with her.

The Departure

SHE WAS GOING TO speak to him.

It was the only logical thing for her to do.

Zaharra needed to get her feelings off her chest, consequences be damned. She needed to know without a shred of doubt whether he felt the same way about her.

And if not, then she would live with her heartbreak and move on.

Decision made, after another restless night of sleep, Zaharra stood outside the shop at her normal time.

She didn't care that Kahr mentioned she should come in later that day; she wanted to talk to him before the morning rush.

Alone and in private.

She pressed her hand against the door and unlocked it. The magic keyed to her aura from the very first day Kahr had hired her.

Her thoughts went back to that day and the way his warm palm had felt over hers when he had activated the spell. It was a simple spell, small magic sold in scrolls by natural-born witches and warlocks.

Once the more advanced spell was attached to the owner of a residence, in this case, Kahr, he could activate the second part of the spell to allow anyone he wanted to lock or unlock the shop.

She pushed the door open, the bell jingling to announce her arrival. The fairy lights were already activated, telling Zaharra that Kahr was up and moving around the shop.

Almost as if summoned, he stepped out of the hallway into the shopfront, his eyebrows crinkling slightly, and Zaharra's gaze immediately went to the travel pack he had slung over his shoulder.

All thought of confessing her feelings went out the window at the sight.

"Are you leaving?" She barely got the words out, her voice cracking.

His intake of breath was sharp, the soft creak of leather from the bag's strap almost deafening against the silence as Kahr shifted again. "I have to go to the port, pick up some more spell scrolls and a few special orders. I usually try to go every few weeks."

"So you leaving suddenly has nothing to do with what happened yesterday?" The words came fast, almost running together.

Kahr stiffened, his grip on the bag tightening.

He averted his gaze, and his voice strained. "Nothing happened yesterday, Zaharra. I'll be back in a week."

Zaharra's jaw dropped as Kahr turned on his heel and walked away.

Sadness filtered through her, only to be chased away by anger. She couldn't believe he had just said that and then walked away.

He had some nerve.

She growled, ready to follow him as the sound of the back door open and closing echoed through the shop. She made it two steps before the jingle of the front door announced someone coming in.

As she spun on her heel, she half expected it to be Kahr returning, and she was more than ready to give him a piece of her mind. "If you think..." The words were already halfway out of her mouth before she realized it wasn't Kahr.

She snapped her mouth shut as Meerek raised an eyebrow at her.

"If you think what???"

Zaharra shook her head as her chest started to ache once more, sadness chasing away her anger.

Meerek took one glance at her face before rushing forward, her arms wrapping around her shoulders and pulling her into a comforting embrace. "Tell me everything."

"You don't have to be here," Zaharra grumbled as she sat behind the counter, going over the accounts book. She side-eyed the special orders book with equal parts disdain and relief. It was the reason Kahr left, and the reason this past week Zaharra had been filtering through her emotions like a hormonal teenager.

"It's been a week, and like I said before, I want to see an interaction between you two," Meerek said over her shoulder before standing on her tiptoes to grab something from a higher shelf.

Zaharra sighed and got up, stomping over to Meerek and taking the glass bottle from her hands. She put it on the shelf, arranging it back into place. "There will be no interaction. I told you, he isn't interested. He made it clear, then left. I'm over it, and him."

Meerek snorted and shook her head before running her finger over a few of the bound notebooks before reaching out to grab a feathered quill.

Zaharra stopped her and leveled a glare her way. "Will you stop touching everything like a child?"

Meerek rolled her eyes and laughed. "I am not the one acting like a child. And from what you said, he most definitely did not make it clear. I just want to see how he acts when he gets back. It's been a week. And you said he would be back around then, right?"

Zaharra gave up and stomped back to the counter. "Yes, and the moment he gets back, I am walking out that door and heading to the pub to get dinner with you. No prolonged interactions."

Meerek waltzed up to the counter and leaned over on her elbows. Zaharra ignored the look her friend was giving her. "You don't know men," Meerek said bluntly, and Zaharra rolled her eyes.

Shaking her head, Meerek grabbed Zaharra's hand. "Roll your eyes all you want, but out of the two of us, I'm the one who dates and flirts and romps and rolls around more than you do. I like men; they are fun. But they are also very dense sometimes. Super thick-headed, and from what you have told me..." She paused and leaned in, making Zaharra lift her gaze. "I think he does like you. I just want to see the way you two interact. I want to see the way he looks at you."

Zaharra slid her hand out from under Meerek's and leaned back in the chair, folding her arms across her chest. She looked down at her feet.

She was wearing the boots Kahr had given her for winning that stupid bet.

They were impractical to wear during the summer. Winter boots trimmed in fur, yet here she was... wearing them like a heart-sick fool, trying to convince Meerek that she wasn't. She kept telling herself she wanted to break them in before winter. When, in reality, she just missed Kahr, and they reminded her of him.

She crossed her arms even tighter, trying to ignore her emotions as they ping-ponged between longing and anger.

Fucking Kahr.

Why did she have to fall for her boss?

Zaharra felt her face heat up before she glared in Meerek's direction. "Like I just said, I'm over it."

"Riiight..." Meerek raised her eyebrows and nodded. "You're a terrible liar. But it's fine. Once he gets back, this whole miscommunication thing that is happening can be solved." She smiled and sauntered over to the other side of the shop. "And I'll be the one to help." She glanced over her shoulder, and Zaharra shook her head.

"Whatever you are about to say, don't. I know that look."

Meerek laughed. "You can thank me at your wedding."

"Oh, my gods and goddess's," Zaharra grumbled and let her head fall back to stare at the ceiling. "You're insane."

The front bells jingled just then, and relief flooded through her. Perfect, a customer to distract her from her mind and Meerek's insane ramblings.

She dropped her head, glancing at the front door, and her relief instantly fled as Kahr stepped into the shop.

A Mentor's Advice

HIS HEART ACHED.

Kahr pressed his hand against his chest as he sat at the table, his mead long forgotten, his food no longer warm. He missed Zaharra and didn't know what to do with this feeling.

Her face, the way it had fallen when he said nothing had happened between them.

Gods...

He reached for his mead and downed the tanker in three gulps.

Gods, he had broken her heart and then just fucking left.

Kahr always tried to do the right thing.

He always stuck to his morals, even though he seemed rigid to some. He had seen through his travels how power, even the smallest amount, could be abused. He had vowed to never be that person. He always wanted to be fair and never hurt those he cared about.

And yet, here he was at the port, running away from a beautiful, kind, charismatic, strong woman who he cared deeply about.

He shook his head.

Zaharra was everything he ever looked for in a partner, and he put himself in a position where he couldn't even be with her without jeopardizing his morals.

Kahr sighed and pushed his tanker away as the tavern maid made her rounds. She dropped another tanker of mead off without a word, and Kahr pulled it across the table, just as a grizzled grey-haired elf slid into the seat across from him.

"Kahr, you look like someone spit on your cupcakes before making you eat them."

He snorted, the achiness in his heart lifting slightly.

His mentor, Ailas, and the person who taught him everything about the realm after he left the Midnight Mountains, had a way with words. It had been about two years since they had seen each other. The port city was good for that though, finding rare goods and long-lost friends when you needed them. It was a type of magic Kahr or anyone else had yet to figure out, but he was glad Ailas was here.

He really needed to talk to someone.

"Well... it kind of feels like that."

Ailas pointed to the plate of cold stew and roasted veggies. Kahr pushed it towards his mentor, and Ailas waved his hand over it, muttering a couple of words. The hair on Kahr's arms stood up for a second as the heavy presence of magic flowed from Ailas's hands. Three seconds later, the food was steaming, and his mentor grabbed a fork.

"So what's their name?" he asked between mouthfuls.

Kahr shook his head and sipped at his mead before placing it back on the table gently. He watched the golden-brown liquid ripple within the tanker, his heart and mind a jumbled mess. "Why do you assume there is someone?"

"Because I can see it in your aura. Your head and heart are at war with each other. Now spill. The magic didn't call me to the port just to sit with my kiddo over food and mead."

Kahr smiled slightly. "Kiddo? Really, Ailas?"

Ailas waved a forkful of food in his direction. "Yes, you might not be a product of my loins, but I took you under my wing and taught you the ways of the realm after I found you wandering about like a lost little duckling."

Kahr grimaced and leaned back into the booth. "Please... please don't ever mention your loins again. Or else this mead is going to come back up."

Ailas raised his eyebrows at Kahr before shoving more food in his mouth.

Kahr sighed and fiddled with the rim of the mead tanker. "Fine, you're right. I just don't know... I don't know what to do. It's complicated."

Ailas moved the fork in a circular motion, signaling Kahr to get to the point.

"I'm her boss."

Ailas finished the mouthful of food. "And?"

Kahr glared at him. "I am her boss. I won't put her in that position."

Ailas sighed and put the fork down, meeting Kahr's glare with an exasperated look. "And what position is that?"

"There is a power dynamic. Between boss and employee, I own the shop she works at. Zaharra needs the money; plus, she is still trying to figure out what she is going to do in life after..." Kahr shook his head. "It doesn't matter. In the end, if I ask to date her, there will always be this expectation. The underlying threat that I could fire her at any point if something doesn't go my way in the relationship."

"Zaharra is a pretty name."

"She is more than just pretty. She is strong, confident, and radiant from the inside out." Kahr chuckled and pulled his hand through his hair. "The first time I met her, she threw me on my ass and...

and I think, no, I know I fell for her in that moment. And in every moment after."

Ailas sighed and wiped his hands with a cloth napkin. "Not everyone thinks the way you do about the power dynamic between people. You had been through a lot by the time I took you under my wing, and your past has made you see things a bit differently. Not that you are wrong. We traveled the same places, have seen how power, even in the smallest form, can be abused. But..." Ailas paused, and Kahr took a deep breath, knowing he was about to get a piece of advice he knew not to ignore. That was something his mentor was good at.

"If she wants to be with you, and you with her, have an open and honest talk. Tell her exactly what you told me. Then work through it. There is always a way without putting anyone's morals in peril. Come up with some solutions together because, right now, you are being selfish and just thinking about yourself. She needs to be included in this decision too. And if you can't, then either the timing is not right, or it was not meant to be."

Kahr sighed, knowing all too well his mentor was right, and reached for his tanker of mead. "I'll tell her when I get back into town."

"That's my boy. Now tell me what you have been up to over these past few years."

Excitement pitted against anxiety within his heart as Kahr walked down the cobbled street towards his shop two days after leaving the port. He could see the lights shining brightly from within, and he took a deep breath.

This was it.

Kahr pushed open the front door, and his heart leapt at the sight of Zaharra sitting behind the counter. Her smile lit up his heart like a flame, only to be snuffed out as her smile faded when she saw it was him.

He definitely deserved that.

"Welcome back." Her voice felt like a bucket of cold water being poured over his head, and it took every ounce of willpower inside of Kahr not to wince. In all the time he had spoken to Zaharra, this icy tone was a new one for him, and he hated it.

"I hope you had a pleasant trip." She picked up a small stack of letters and held them out to him. "The courier stopped by yesterday to drop these off."

Kahr stepped forward, never taking his eyes off Zaharra's face, and reached for the letters. He didn't even spare Zaharra's friend, Meerek, a single glance as she stood there. Good, let there be witnesses, he didn't want to hide what needed to be said.

"Zaharra, I wanted to…" He paused as his thumb drifted over a very familiar seal on the letter he was holding.

Kahr felt his stomach drop, his skin flushing with heat, and he gulped, looking down.

"You wanted what?" Zaharra asked.

"I… I just…" Kahr couldn't concentrate as he read the looping letters on the top envelope.

Good gods, it was a summons.

Not fucking now, of all the times…

"Right," Zaharra sighed. "I'll just be going, then. See you tomorrow, I guess."

Kahr snapped his head up and watched as Zaharra stepped around the counter and gave him much more room than necessary as she stalked towards the door. Meerek ran after her, catching the door before it slammed shut.

Kahr dropped his head, his heart breaking into a million pieces.

"I wish that were true," he whispered.

Gone

Her blood was boiling her from the inside out.

That was the only accurate word Zaharra could use to describe how she was feeling. She slammed the front door open, stomping out onto the cobblestone street, and turned right. Her vision blurred, her face and eyes on fire as she ground her jaw.

"What are you doing?" Meerek whisper-yelled behind her and grabbed at her arm, pulling her to a stop.

Zaharra stared straight ahead, sucking in a deep, ragged breath through her nose. "Fucking going home. I think that interaction was quite clear."

"Clear... clear... I'm sorry, but that man wants you."

Zaharra scoffed and took another step forward, and another. Meerek tugged at her arm to stop her, but Zaharra had trained to be a fighter her whole life.

Meerek was no match in trying to hold her in place.

Her best friend sighed and let go, before dashing around to place her body in front of Zaharra.

She stopped again, unwilling to run her over.

"You couldn't see it. The way he looked at you and the way you looked at him. I don't know what his hang-up is, but you need to talk to him. This miscommunication bullshit is just that, bullshit."

Zaharra shook her head, eyes burning from unshed tears. Her jaw clenched so hard, she swore a tooth cracked. After a few deep breaths, she finally looked at her friend. "He wasn't even able to talk to me, or look at me, after I handed him his letters. For a moment, it was like maybe there was something, but then... No, I'm over it. There is no miscommunication, Meerek. I'm done. And I'm going home and going to sleep. I am exhausted."

She stepped around Meerek, unable to hold back her tears as she ran all the way home.

Her eyes were grainy, and her head pounded something fierce as Zaharra stared up at the barn ceiling. Wasn't it just a week ago that she was in this same headspace? Her mind a tumbling mess about her boss and her life and what in the world she was supposed to be doing with it.

She waited for the anxiety to come, but it didn't, her body too numb and exhausted from bawling her eyes out all night. She scrubbed at her face and willed her body to sit up.

This wasn't her way.

Zaharra had never run before. She always stomped towards her problems and right through them.

And yet, ever since she got back home, she had been running. Running away from the fact she was in love with her boss and running away from the fact that she would have to find something new to do with her life.

No, it was time she spoke to Kahr. And if that ended in disaster, she would march herself right into another job.

Her heart ached at the thought of leaving the shop, but she had to do this.

If only for her sanity.

A few minutes in the shower dulled the pounding in her head and washed away the graininess in her eyes. Zaharra dressed quickly, reaching for the boots out of habit. She paused and sighed, choosing to wear her sandals instead.

She didn't need to wear the boots anymore; they were broken in and she didn't want to explain to Kahr why she was wearing winter boots in the height of summer. Definitely since the answer was because she missed him.

With her sandals on, she was almost at the door when she turned around and grabbed the boots. Fine, she would take them with her. Just to throw them at Kahr's head if their talk went south.

Zaharra snorted before shaking her head and putting them next to the door. No, that would be immature, and she wanted to have an adult conversation.

Growling low under her breath, she kicked off her sandals, before finding a breathable pair of socks and lacing up the boots. Damn it all, but she liked the boots. They were cute and functional, and screw it if it was summer. And screw it if she was wearing them because they made her think about her boss.

Plus, kicking is easier in boots than sandals... not like she was going to be kicking anyone. But if she had too...

"Gods... enough procrastinating," she whispered to herself before opening the barn door and stepping outside into light grey skies. Soft blues and pinks peeked through, and Zaharra knew if she turned right instead of left, in five minutes, she would be at her favorite tree, which she could climb and watch the sun rise.

And continue procrastinating a conversation she really needed to have.

Instead, she turned left, and her long strides ate up the dirt road away from the barn. She reached the main cobblestones within minutes. Her heart raced, anxiety threatening to rear its nasty head. She took a deep breath and forged ahead, not noticing the racing figure in front of her until they almost collided.

Zaharra skidded to a halt just in time to catch Meerek. Her friend panted, waving a letter in her hand. "It's ... I ... I was..." She sucked in a deep breath and folded in half.

"Are you okay? Why are you running? You know you don't run."

Meerek barked out a breathy rasp, and Zaharra wasn't sure if her friend was laughing or dying at the moment.

"It has your name on it. I... I saw... saw it, oh fuck, I can't breathe... It was on the shop door," Meerek panted.

Zaharra frowned and took the letter. Who would be sending her letters at her place of work?

Her face flushed, heart beating furiously as she read her name on the front, scrawled in handwriting she knew all too well.

Kahr had written her a letter.

Then left it pinned to the shop door, making sure she would see it.

She ripped it open and read, her eyes scanning its contents faster than she ever thought was possible.

What the...

"Oh, fuck no," she yelled and crumpled the letter, throwing it to the ground. "Absolutely the fuck not."

She took off at a run, heading towards the shop. She barely skidded to a halt before slamming her hand down on the door handle. The magic activated, unlocking the door, and she threw it wide open, stomping inside.

"Kahr... where the fuck are you? You don't just get to leave a note like that and just ... just.... I'm going to... ahgggg!" She screamed in frustration as she bounded up the stairs and threw his bedroom door open. It bounced off the wall, but Zaharra was already turning around and stomping down the stairs. She threw open the spare room door before heading towards the back storage. By the time she emerged to the front of the shop, Meerek had shown up, gasping for air, crumpled letter in hand.

"He is fucking gone," Zaharra yelled.

Meerek's eyes widened as Zaharra stomped by her and grabbed a travel bag from the shopfront.

"What are you... what are you doing?" Meerek gasped.

Zaharra grabbed a few pairs of cold-weather leggings and tunics, along with essential travel gear. She shoved it all into the pack before turning around to look for rope. You always needed rope.

That was something her mother drilled into her from an early age.

Rope and a good blade were essential in any situation.

She snagged a decent bundle of rope and tied it to the travel pack before grabbing one of the newer hatchets she had her eyes on to buy later in the month.

Fuck it.

She would pay for all this stuff later.

Zaharra turned towards her still-panting best friend. "Put all this shit on my tab. You're in charge until I get back. I have a goliath to hunt down."

The Wild Goliath Hunt

"I DON'T KNOW WHEN I'll be back, Zaharra. I might be gone for a season, or maybe a year, or even longer, but I wanted to let you know... blah blah blah," Zaharra grumbled as she adjusted her travel pack.

Taking a deep breath, she looked up... and up, and up. The Midnight Mountains loomed before her, permanently snow-capped peaks caressing clear blue skies. Zaharra wasn't sure how far she would have to go to find Kahr, but Goddess help her, if she had to, she would go to the very top of the highest peak to find him.

Just to slap him on the back of the head and tell him he was stupid... and how dare he leave after saying he would never forget their time spent together.

Zaharra closed her eyes and took a deep breath, letting the cold air coat her lungs. She had barely crossed the border between the plains to the mountains an hour ago. Even though it was summer, it was still cold in the mountains and she knew soon she would eventually reach snow. But right now, she was standing on a narrow, well-worn trail weaving its path through a field of wildflowers. She was also sweating like crazy even with the cold breeze. Dropping her pack unceremoniously in front of her, she stripped off her long-sleeved tunic and wrapped it around her waist.

Lifting her water bag to her lips, she took a few swallows before eyeing the fork in the path before her. Both paths led up the mountain, both equally worn, and neither looked like someone, especially a stupid goliath, had used them recently. So now she had to figure out if she should take the path that led up the east side of the mountain or the west side.

Zaharra grumbled and squatted down, looking at the paths at a different angle. She really didn't need much, just a crushed flower, or scuffed dirt from a shoe, a small, upturned rock.... Anything, really.

She shook her head and stood up. It looked like she was just going to pick a path and hope for the best. What she really needed at the moment was a sign, something that said *Hey, Kahr went this way a few hours ago.*

Zaharra snorted and bent to pick up her pack, ready to restart her wild goliath hunt as a bird swooped down, attacking the ground a mere two feet away from her.

A shrill scream echoed through the air, causing Zaharra to slap her hands against her ears. "What in the goddess is that noise?" she shouted, looking around.

The high-pitched shrieking continued, and she followed the sound, shooing away the bird still attacking the ground near a cluster of small flowers. Getting on all fours, Zaharra's eyes widened as she took in the small, huddled form of a fairy.

"Oh, hey," she whispered. "It's safe now. I shooed the big, mean bird away."

The fairy lowered its hands, its little eyes widening as it stared at Zaharra. "It's gone? You made it go away?" the fairy asked, its voice light and airy.

Zaharra nodded. "I did."

The fairy unfolded from its huddled position and stood up, glancing around Zaharra to the sky. It stood no bigger than four inches, iridescent wings slowly fluttering back and forth. The fairy was wearing a bright yellow tunic with dark trousers. It's hair, a mousy dark brown to match its eyes. "Hmmm..." It looked at her, narrowing its eyes. "Thank you, I think."

Zaharra raised her eyebrows. "You think? Did you want to get eaten by a bird?"

The fairy rolled its eyes, reminding Zaharra of her little brothers. "I wasn't going to get eaten. I have a sword, see!"

Zaharra went cross-eyed, staring at the sharp metal sewing needle currently pointed at her nose. She couldn't help the snort that escaped, and the fairy jumped backwards, its wings fluttering to keep it upright.

"Sorry...sorry. Of course, I shouldn't have involved myself. Clearly, you had things handled."

The fairy sheathed its needle and nodded. "Yes, so..."

A shadow fell over them, and Zaharra glanced up to see a few birds circling overhead. When she looked back, the fairy was gone.

"What? Where did you go?"

She felt a tug at one of her small braids decorating her hair and Zaharra turned her head to see the fairy holding on for dear life. Sighing, she got to her feet, careful not to jostle the fairy currently making its home in her hair. "All right, well, you can stick with me, I guess. But I'm going further into the mountains. Also, my name is Zaharra, in case you wanted to know."

The fairy sighed, settling in on Zaharra's shoulder, its small hand still wrapped around her braid. "My name is Arina. But everyone just calls me Ari. I'm on my rite of passage journey into womanhood and adulthood, I guess. I'm also kind of blowing it."

Zaharra sucked in a deep breath, as Ari's words hit a little too deep. "Oof, I know how that feels, Ari. I kind of failed mine too."

"Oh! Are you also on your rite of passage journey too?"

She went to shake her head before stopping, remembering she now had a fairy holding on to her hair. "No, orcs go to the queen's city for our rite of passage and do a bunch of tests, to figure out what they want to do with the rest of their life. But I already knew what I wanted, and... it just wasn't meant to be. That was four-ish weeks ago now."

"Oh," Ari whispered. "What did you want to do? Why can't you do it?"

Zaharra gritted her teeth and sucked in a deep breath. Well, she did open herself up for that question. "I was supposed to be part of the queen's guard. A family legacy, really. My mom, grandmom, and her mom before her were all part of the queen's guard. And I... I..." She choked slightly and sucked in a breath.

Ari made a slight noise, akin to a coo, and she felt the fairy stroke her cheek slightly. Zaharra closed her eyes and took another breath. "Sorry, I don't mean to be such a downer, definitely not when you are out on your own journey. But long story short, it was decided I would be better off doing something else."

"Well, that is stupid." Ari huffed, making Zaharra chuckle slightly.

"Yes, well... that was how my rite of passage went. How about you? What makes you think you are failing?"

Ari grumbled something under her breath.

"I didn't hear that."

"Uhgggg... fine. For our tribe's rite of passage, we are supposed to go on an epic adventure and be all heroic and shit. Bring back stories to tell the elders, and I've done nothing. Nothing!" Ari yelled the last part and Zaharra winced slightly. "Sorry... it's just that I can't go back until I've completed my adventure, and I miss home."

"I'm sorry. I'm guessing you fighting that bird would have counted as epic?"

Ari shrugged. "Epic, yes. Heroic and an adventure... I'm not sure. Probably not, but who are we kidding? That bird would have eaten me if you hadn't saved me."

This time, Zaharra shrugged, causing Ari to lift off her shoulder, wings flapping almost too fast for her to see.

Ari glared at her, and Zaharra laughed. "Get back on my shoulder. I'm going to help you get your story to bring back to the elders."

"You are?" Ari chirped and settled back onto her shoulder, this time sitting down.

"Yes. But first, I am looking for someone. Did you see a goliath come this way?"

"Oh, yup, like super early. The sun had just risen. He went that way." Ari pointed to the path heading east up the mountain. "Why are you looking for a goliath?"

Zaharra picked up her travel pack and settled the strap across her chest, and the shoulder Ari wasn't sitting on. "That, my dear fairy companion, is a long story."

Reunion

THE COLD AIR NIPPED at Kahr's face as he lifted his gaze to the sky. It was almost midday, and he only just reached the uppermost valley. He had chosen the eastern trail up the mountains because it would cut his trip by two days, but he had forgotten how steep the terrain was. And that the eastern side already had snow, even in the heart of summer.

He took a deep breath, letting the cool air coat his lungs. It had been a long time since he had tasted the air of his homeplace. The crisp air brought along the scent of evergreens and dried dirt, even though if he opened his eyes, all he would see at the moment would be snow and rocky mountainsides.

Kahr opened his eyes as a bittersweet sadness rolled through him. He hated himself for leaving. He had lingered briefly at his shop, wondering if he should just ignore the summons from the elders. He knew the consequences, though. Banishment... and not just from the clan.

No, the summons was laced with magic, and if he ignored it, a mark would appear, tattooed across his entire body. Any goliath he would ever interact with in the future would see the mark and stay away, lest they suffer banishment as well.

It would mean never seeing his sister again, never going into the Midnight Mountains again, and it would mark him as a coward.

And most importantly, Kahr knew Zaharra could never love a coward.

He took a deep breath and grabbed his travel bag, ready to get this summons over with before pausing and cocking his head slightly.

What in the realm?

He turned as voices rang out behind him, one voice in particular he knew all too well.

Zaharra.

His jaw went slack as he watched the gorgeous orc zero in on him and increase her stride. She wore a scowl as her long legs ate up the space between them until she was in his face, finger pointed right at him.

"How dare you!"

"I... why..." Kahr stumbled on his words, still in disbelief that Zaharra was right in front of him.

"No, you don't get to talk right now," Zaharra yelled. "I get to talk, so shut it."

Kahr's eyes widened, but he complied, still not knowing why she was here, chasing him up a mountainside. She dropped her bag, and Kahr was struck with disbelief once more as a fairy lifted off her shoulder and buzzed straight up to his face.

"Ya!" the fairy yelled and pointed a sewing needle at him. "You shut it and let Z talk."

"Ari, I got this. Please don't poke him in the eye with your sword," Zaharra grumbled.

The fairy, Ari, glared at Kahr for a moment before sheathing its sewing needle, or from what Zaharra just said, its sword. Kahr almost laughed at the absurdity of what was happening, but the look on Zaharra's face stopped him.

"You left." She pulled out a piece of paper and waved it in the air. "You left without saying goodbye. This... this letter is not going to cut it."

Kahr opened his mouth to speak.

"No, I'm not finished," Zaharra yelled and crumpled his letter into a ball and threw it at him.

Kahr snapped his mouth shut as the letter hit him square in the face.

"You don't get to run away. You don't get to say that you don't know when, or if, you will ever be back." Zaharra's face fell slightly as she choked on her words.

"Zaharra." Kahr sighed and shook his head. "The—"

She held out her hand in a stopping motion, and Kahr shut his mouth again for what seemed like the hundredth time.

"I'll admit it. When I first came back to the village, I was a fucking mess. I didn't know what to do with myself or my life, and I still don't. And I understand I am just your employee, but I can't think about... I can't fathom working at your shop without you there. I know you don't like me the way I like you." Zaharra sucked in a deep breath and plowed on. "Because I like you, Kahr, I really do. But I can live with it if you only see me as someone who works for you. What I can't live with is not seeing you ever again. Every time I'm with you... it's like... it feels like home, and I can't give that up. I needed you to know that."

Kahr felt Zaharra's confession like a sucker punch straight to his gut. Before he could think, before he could talk himself out of his next move, Kahr stepped forward and wrapped his arms around her.

A startled gasp flew out of her as he pulled her close and lowered his head, capturing her lips with his.

Kissing Zaharra was everything he had expected and more.

She parted her lips, and Kahr deepened the kiss, barely registering as Zaharra wrapped her arms around him. He thrust a hand into her hair, and she moaned into his mouth. The small amount of control Kahr still had within him snapped, and he lifted her up, trying to get even closer. He felt her strong legs wrap around his waist before he knelt, bringing them both to the ground.

At that moment, she was all he could think about. The way she whimpered as he pulled back from the kiss to nibble at her lips. The way her hands felt digging into his shoulders. The way her head fell back and the ragged sigh she made as he kissed his way across her jaw and down her neck. The way she arched in his hands, her body pressing against his as he captured her lips again, this time his tongue exploring the inside of her mouth.

She was fucking perfect, and he needed more. He needed to taste more of her, touch every single inch of her, and it felt like he had all the time in the world and yet no time at all.

An annoying buzzing at his ear and high-pitched chattering pulled him out of his bliss, and Kahr broke the kiss, snarling at whatever insect was distracting him.

He blinked rapidly at the red-faced fairy, who was yelling at both Zaharra and him and gesturing wildly about. He concentrated on trying to make out the fairy's high-pitched screaming.

"You are going to cause a fucking snow slide, you stupid, big oafs. Stop trying to crawl inside each other's pants out here in the middle of the mountains! You're both so loud with all the moaning and growling and you need to go find a cave so I don't have to rip out my eyes after you traumatize me with all *this*." Ari gestured wildly with her hands, motioning to all of Zaharra and him.

Zaharra's breathy laugh echoed out beneath him, and Kahr glanced down with a smile before shaking his head and lifting off of her. He reached down and pulled her up, out of the snow and back into his arms, right where she belonged. Pushing the hair away from her face, he tucked one of the smaller braids behind her ear before cupping her cheek.

"I'm sorry I didn't do that sooner. I'm sorry I just left, thinking that a letter would have sufficed. And I'm sorry I didn't tell you the moment that we first met that I fell for you, quite literally. I had every intention of asking you out the very next day, but then you came into the shop and demanded a job from me. Then I became your boss, and I couldn't just come on to you, it would have been so inappropriate. But as hard as I tried to keep my attraction and feelings at bay, they just grew."

Kahr rested his forehead against Zaharra's and tightened his hold on her.

She pulled away slightly and narrowed her eyes at him. "Wait, are you telling me the reason you never made a move on me was because you're my boss?"

Your Rope or Mine

Zaharra couldn't believe it.

The only reason Kahr hadn't told her how he felt sooner was because he thought it was inappropriate, because he was her boss.

"I didn't want to take advantage. So yes, the reason I didn't tell you how I felt about you is because I was your boss. I felt it—"

Zaharra pressed her fingers against his lips, shutting him up. "Wait, what do you mean, *was* your boss?"

Kahr raised an eyebrow before nipping at her fingers.

Heat flashed through her body, her heart beating faster, and Zaharra gulped slightly. She watched as Kahr smirked before grabbing her hand off his mouth. "You didn't read my entire letter, did you, sweetheart?"

Her face heated instantly, and Zaharra knew she was blushing. "I mean... I... I kind of..." she stammered as Kahr's smirk turned into a full-on smile. She glowered as he chuckled.

"Fine, damn it. I never got past the part of you possibly not returning before I raided the shop for gear and left Meerek in charge. I wasn't exactly thinking straight."

Kahr pulled her closer, wrapping his free arm around her waist, and murmured, "I gave you the shop. Put it in your name in case I never got the chance to return."

"What?" Zaharra said, completely entranced by Kahr's piercing blue eyes. She could feel her own heartbeat, could feel how it matched the beat of Kahr's. "Wait...what? You did what?" His words finally registered, and Zaharra shook her head. "What do you mean, you put the shop in my name?"

"You're the owner."

Zaharra widened her eyes. "Are you serious right now? You gave me the shop."

Kahr nodded. "You're the owner now. To do with it as you please. I wanted to make sure you were taken care of in case I didn't make it back."

Zaharra shook her head. "No. No ifs, Kahr. You're coming back, even if I have to drag you down this mountain myself."

Kahr shook his head and kissed her palm. "Well, because you said so, I'll definitely be coming back.

But I think you missed the point. I am no longer your boss."

"I am my own boss," Zaharra whispered and grinned. "And you are technically unemployed. Just a poor, wandering goliath. Whatever will we do with you?" Kahr chuckled as she pushed away from him slightly and shrugged. "I guess I could offer you a job at this newly acquired trader's shop of mine, but it did just come to my attention that employers and employees shouldn't date. So that's a bit of a—"

Zaharra squealed as Kahr lunged towards her and scooped her up in his arms. She wrapped her legs around his waist as he kissed her hard on the lips before pulling away and slapping her ass playfully. "You're being a brat."

This time, Zaharra laughed so hard it echoed throughout the valley. Kahr laughed along with her until a low rumble overshadowed them.

She glanced up at the bright blue sky and her brow furrowed. "Was that... thunder? I don't see any clouds."

Ari appeared from seemingly nowhere, and Zaharra winced, being so caught up with Kahr that she forgot all about her little fairy friend. "Maybe it's the snow slide I told you big, stupid oafs you would cause from being so loud. Serves you right for not listening to me."

"Ari is right. It could be a snowslide. The snow is fresh, and this valley is prone to them. But there is a storm heading our way. I can taste it on the wind. The clouds probably haven't reached us yet. Either way, we should get moving. There is a shelter on the other side of the valley. We can reach it in a few hours," Kahr stated, but he didn't let her go. Instead, he gripped her tighter.

Zaharra wiggled slightly, and Kahr looked her straight in the eyes, his face dead serious. "Don't do that."

She smiled and wiggled again. "Don't do what?"

"Wiggle like that when I'm holding you."

"Why?"

Kahr took a deep breath and clenched his jaw. "You know exactly why, sweetheart, and I don't think we would want to traumatize poor Ari with the things I would do to you if you wiggle like that one more time."

Zaharra pressed her lips together, suppressing a smirk, and loosened her legs from around Kahr's waist. He slowly lowered her to the ground, keeping her body pressed to his.

"Uhggg... finally," Ari muttered as Zaharra stepped back and grabbed her travel pack. Kahr did the same and Ari zipped between the two of them before flying ahead. He took her hand, just as another rumble echoed through the valley, and Zaharra swore the ground shook slightly.

"Do you see anything, Ari?" Zaharra called out.

Ari zipped back and up, buzzing around in a circle before coming back down to eye level.

"There are some clouds rolling in on the east-most side of the mountain. I didn't see any snow moving, so it might just be the storm like Kahr said."

Kahr nodded, his eyebrows slightly pinched together as he pulled Zaharra forward to follow him. "We need to get over the ledge before the storm hits. It's dangerous when icy."

The clouds rolled over the valley, bringing with them a dusting of snow. The snowflakes were small, dancing through the air with the breeze. They had both stopped to put on long-sleeved wool outer layers along with hats and gloves. When the snow started, Ari tucked herself within the top of Zaharra's pack, grumbling about her wings freezing together.

As the wind picked up, blowing harder, Kahr stopped and stepped to the side, releasing her hand. "The shelter I'm thinking of is right on the other side of the ledge. Like I said, it can be dangerous when icy."

The ledge in question was ten inches wide at most, getting smaller near the middle, only to widen out at the end, and part of a rocky outcropping attached to the side of the mountain. What looked like thick metal hooks decorated the mountain side, but they were few and far between the further the outcropping went. Below the outcropping, the valley dropped off about fifteen feet. Just far enough of a drop to injure oneself but still survive.

"Dangerous when icy... Kahr, it looks dangerous all the time. Why risk walking the ledge, when you can lower yourself down the fifteen feet, walk across, then climb out?"

Kahr pulled Zaharra into a side hug. "It's deceptive. It might look like a fifteen-foot drop, but even during the summer, the ground is covered with at least three feet of snow. Not only that, but..." He paused and reached up, cupping her jaw and angling her head just so. He lowered his head down to her eye level. "Right there. Do you see the snow slightly shifting about halfway across?"

Zaharra squinted, looking for what he was describing. It took her a moment, but she found it. "The snow looks like it's moving... getting lower, almost."

"That's because it is. The snow hides cracks in the rocks. Some are only a few feet deep, while others are seemingly endless. Here in the mountains, we call valleys like this Ebon Hallow's."

Zaharra shivered slightly. "Ebon, as in the god who protects the gateway into the afterlife?"

"Correct, and while I know where a few of the cracks and fissures are, I haven't seen this valley in over ten years. I'm not willing to chance it, or you. Which is why the ledge is the safer choice."

"It's so weird that in all my studies, I never learned about... well, now that I think about it, I was never really taught anything about the Midnight Mountains." Zaharra eyed the valley and the ledge, along with the sides of the mountain, with even more curiosity. "I mean, it's the closest mountain range to the plains, but..."

Kahr shifted slightly. "Not a lot of travelers come this way. Most never take the eastern path up the mountains and goliaths rarely leave their mountain homes."

"Still, I wish I knew more about your people and home." Zaharra shook her head as the snow flurries intensified along with the wind. "We should probably hurry. The storm is getting worse."

"I'll teach you all about the mountains and goliaths once we get over the ledge."

Zaharra leaned her head back and placed a quick kiss on Kahr's chin before squirming out of his hold and pulling off her travel pack.

"So, will we be using your rope or mine?"

The Ledge

KAHR WASN'T THE LEAST bit surprised that Zaharra came prepared. He even noted the hatchet strapped to her pack, the one end sporting a razor-sharp pick, which would be perfect when traversing the ledge. There was a tricky spot halfway across they might need it for.

He took off his pack and pulled out a thick coil of rope. "We are going to use both. You know how to make a climbing harness, right?"

Zaharra nodded. "Along with some basic rappelling knots."

Kahr smiled. "Good. Go ahead and make your harness. We will attach our two ropes together. Then I'll go first. The first and last parts are pretty easy. The middle is the trickiest part."

Zaharra was quick with her harness, and after checking it, Kahr deemed it fit before attaching the two of them together. Zaharra watched intently as Kahr weaved the ropes together. "It's called a double grapevine knot. It's complicated, but when done properly, whatever you tie together will not come undone. Here, try it."

He handed the section of rope over to her, and she tugged at it. "That's pretty handy. Will you teach me how to do it?"

Kahr nodded as the wind increased, the snow pelting down sideways. "Of course, but we need to get going. The storm is only going to get worse. Just remember, if you slip, don't panic. Use the pick end of your hatchet, if need be, and I'll be with you the entire way."

Zaharra smirked. "Same. If you fall, I'll catch you."

He inhaled slightly and drew Zaharra into his arms. "You already did."

Zaharra smiled and wrapped her arms around his neck. "Awwww."

"Seriously, I might as well brave the cold and freeze my wings off just to get away from you two. It's nauseating." Ari's shrill voice echoed from Zaharra's pack, followed by fake gagging.

Kahr rolled his eyes. "Let's get going before the ledge freezes over."

Zaharra snorted and pulled away, bouncing her travel pack on her shoulders a few times and eliciting a small shriek from inside.

"Rude!" Ari's muffled voice echoed from Zaharra's pack.

Kahr smiled and shook his head as Zaharra grabbed the coiled-up rope from his hands and tugged him towards the cliff. "After you, old man."

"Old!" Kahr laughed as he started edging out onto the ledge. He grabbed the end of the rope from Zaharra, and she gave him a little more slack so he could feed it over the first metal hook.

"Yes, old. How else would I have caught up to you hiking the mountain?" she shouted over the wind as Kahr continued placing one careful step in front of the other.

At the second hook, he looped the rope over it. When he glanced back to make sure Zaharra removed the rope from the first hook, she raised her eyebrows at him. "I know what I'm doing. You don't have to worry."

"I was just checking, sweetheart," Kahr said, as he continued moving. "And as for your comment, maybe I was just walking slow because the thought of leaving you was akin to torture."

Zaharra blushed, and Kahr reached out, cupping her cheek. She gazed at him with her beautiful amber eyes, and his heart squeezed a little before he dropped his hand and continued moving across the ledge.

She stayed silent behind him as the middle of the ledge loomed closer. He might have said the ledge was the safer of the two options, but even Kahr had to admit that once you gazed upon the middle of the ledge, traversing an Ebon Hallow looked a lot more appealing.

Kahr stopped. "All right. Not sure if you can see…"

"See the nothingness? Yes, I see absolutely no ledge. You didn't say the middle was a four-foot gap, Kahr," Zaharra grumbled.

Kahr smirked. "It's okay to be scared."

A smarting pain lanced through his arm as Zaharra punched him, and he laughed. "I'm not scared. Just tell me how we are getting over this gap without falling down a cliff face and breaking our legs," Zaharra growled.

He shrugged off his pack and handed it to Zaharra, who was still eyeing the gap. She took it without question as he looped more rope onto a hook and gave himself some slack.

"We are jumping." Kahr rushed his words and leapt before Zaharra could say anything, landing without incident. He turned and tried not to smile at the horrified, yet angry look plastered across Zaharra's face. He reached out his arm. "Throw my pack and your pack over."

"You're not throwing meeee!"

Ari zipped out of Zaharra's pack and landed on her shoulder with a huff. She grabbed hold of one of Zaharra's smaller braids and leaned into the warmth of her neck as the wind buffeted against them.

"That was a dick move. Not telling me you were jumping until you did. I should drop your pack into the ravine below."

He smiled. "I'll make it up to you once we get to the shelter. And I promise not to scare you again."

"Wasn't scared," Zaharra grumbled before tossing him his pack. Once he put it on, she tossed hers over before turning her head and whispering something to Ari.

Ari shook her head, and Zaharra sighed before rolling her shoulders and launching herself through the air.

The moment Zaharra landed, Kahr reached out, tugging her closer as her back foot slipped a little. "See, that wasn't so bad. The rest of the ledge is easy after that."

Zaharra shrugged her pack on and narrowed her eyes at him. "Sure, I'll believe you once we get to the other side."

They reached the end of the ledge without incident, or any surprises, just as he had promised. Getting Zaharra out of her harness though proved to be more of an ordeal than the ledge. Kahr couldn't stop laughing as he tried helping her. The rope had somehow twisted around her thighs and upper torso at the same time when she tried to take it off.

"This is not funny. I am freezing, and I am tired, and I am mad. And if I could kick you right now, I would!" Zaharra yelled as she shook and wiggled her body, trying to escape.

"Stop moving. You're making it worse." Kahr wheezed, barely able to take a full breath from laughing so hard, as Zaharra continued jumping up and down.

"I swear. In all my training, I never got stuck in a rope harness until you came along."

Kahr doubled over in laughter as the wind picked up, dusting them both in snow and throwing Zaharra into him. He grabbed her, saving them both from toppling over into the snow.

"Okay. Okay, let's just get to the shelter and get you warm. Then we can get you out of the mess you got yourself into."

Zaharra glared at him and shook her hair out of her face. "And how in all the realms am I getting to the shelter when I'm trussed up like a bale of hay?"

"Like this." Kahr grabbed the jumbled-up mess of rope at Zaharra's middle and slung her over his shoulder.

Shelter from the Storm

"WAIT!" ZAHARRA SQUEALED AS she flew and landed on Kahr's broad shoulder.

"Nope. You're cold and the storm is getting worse. We have to get going."

Kahr wrapped his arm around her hips, holding Zaharra in place, and grabbed their bags with his free hand.

Zaharra huffed, slightly from embarrassment, but also from the fact that Kahr was right. The snow had turned from small flurries to almost blizzard conditions. The wind was icy and sharp against her face. She let her head hang down, burying her face against Kahr's lower back to keep the chill away.

Never in her life had Zaharra been slung over someone's shoulder and carried like a sack of potatoes. She could imagine what Meerek would have to say in this situation. Probably something along the lines of how Kahr could handle her in other ways.

She groaned, and Kahr tightened his hold on her hips.

"Sorry, sweetheart, we are almost there. Then I'll get you right side up again."

Yes, that was why she was groaning. Not because she was thinking about Kahr's hands on her body, and the way he had been calling her *sweetheart* after they kissed for the first time. And every time after.

Zaharra shivered, thinking about the way Kahr's mouth had felt on hers and the way her body reacted.

"And we're here."

She lifted her head as the wind suddenly died out. They had entered a small overhang, and she twisted slightly, trying to get a better view of their dim surroundings as Kahr continued walking.

He bent slightly, a scrape sounding to Zaharra's right, and she twisted that way to see he had put the bags down. She squinted, trying to see through the darkness in front of Kahr, but she couldn't make anything out.

"So, are you going to put me down, or...?"

"Shit, sorry. Yes."

He pulled her forward and her feet hit the ground with a soft, echoing thud. Her body shivered again.

Being pressed this close to Kahr's body was doing insane things to her.

"Right. Fire. Let's get you warmed up. But first..."

Kahr leaned over, grabbing his bedroll out of his bag and laid it out on the ground. "Work on trying to get yourself free while I make us a fire."

"Right." Zaharra nodded as Kahr helped her sit on his bedroll. She bit her lower lip as he walked off, already missing his warm presence. With a sigh, she looked down at the impossible mess of ropes tangled around her body and got to work.

A few moments of tugging and a couple of curse words later, she found where the whole mess had started and began untangling herself. Ari zipped out of her bag and onto her shoulder as she stood and stretched, popping her back. "Well, let's pray I never have to do that again. Right, Ari?"

"Are you and Kahr going to have sex?"

"What! You... what? Why would you..." Zaharra tripped over her words as Ari flew off her shoulder to hover in front of her face.

She shrugged. "Because you like each other and can't stop kissing."

Zaharra felt her face flush slightly as she heard Kahr's footsteps approaching.

He flicked his hand at Ari slightly with a scowl on his face. "Go explore the rest of the shelter."

"That was a little rude," Zaharra said as Ari zipped away into the flickering darkness, the light of the fire slowly growing brighter.

Kahr looked at her, his gaze intense as he blocked her view of everything but him. He cupped the back of her head, fingers threading through her hair before pressing his body into hers.

"Zaharra," he rumbled, his gaze intense.

She swore her heart skipped a beat as her hands ran up the front of his shirt to rest on his shoulders. "Yes?"

"Don't pay any attention to what Ari asked. We don't have to sleep together tonight or any time soon. I want to make it absolutely clear that I am content not taking this, us, any farther than you are comfortable with. You are fully in control of this relationship."

Her stomach dipped, her knees weakening as an all-too-familiar ache started between her legs. Damn it to the gods, but what he just said made Zaharra want to rip his clothes off right then and there.

She clenched her hands, gripping his shoulders, and licked her lips. "And if I do?"

"Do what?"

Kahr's voice dipped an octave, eliciting another shiver from her. She leaned in slightly, her lips almost touching his.

"Want to sleep with you? Right here, right now."

She wasn't sure who moved first, only that their lips collided and Kahr was kissing her, and it felt like it had before.

Intense, overwhelming, and so sinfully good.

Seconds later, her back hit the stone wall, Kahr's hands running down her sides to cup her ass and lift her off the ground. She wrapped her legs around his waist, running her hands through his hair.

She gasped slightly as he broke the kiss to suck on her bottom lip, his hands solid against her hips, holding her against the wall as he slowly ground into her.

Her hands ran down his neck and back, nails digging into the infuriating clothes he was still wearing.

Kahr growled and reached up to grasp the side of her neck, his thumb running over her bottom lip. He rested his forehead against hers, his breathing ragged.

"Why did you stop?" she whispered in confusion.

He opened his eyes, the flames from the fire casting a sinful glow over his face as he kissed her gently. "Before we go any farther, you should know I'm on a fertility elixir, so we don't have to worry about any accidents happening. If we even take it that far tonight."

Zaharra sucked in a breath. "Oh... I, I didn't even think about that. Um, I'm not exactly... I don't..." Damn it, she was babbling and ruining the moment.

"As long as one person is taking the elixir, it's fine. I just wanted to put your mind at ease," Kahr whispered as he kissed her again, gentler this time.

She groaned, grinding her hips into his before sliding her hands down, tugging at the bottom of his shirt.

Kahr took a step back and turned, laying them both down on the bedroll. He lifted an arm over his head and grasped his shirt, pulling it over his head and throwing it to the side.

"Was that what you wanted, sweetheart?"

She nodded and bit her lip as she gazed at Kahr's magnificent chest, wanting nothing more than to run her hands over his warm skin and thick muscles. He leaned over her, placing both hands on either side of her head and closing his eyes as Zaharra reached up, smoothing her hands up his stomach, nails scraping over his chest.

His groan fueled her desire as she continued exploring his bare skin. She dug her nails in, eliciting a moan from Kahr, and he bent at the elbows, bringing his weight down on her. As she arched into him, he took her mouth again.

She ground her hips into his, a frustrated growl coming forth as Zaharra realized she was still fully dressed, and Kahr was still wearing pants.

She broke the kiss. "I need us to be naked, like, yesterday. I don't want to wait any longer."

Kahr growled and kissed her hard before pulling back and grabbing her hands from his back, pinning them above her head.

She gasped slightly as he ground his hips into hers, mimicking the move she had done earlier before whispering in her ear. "Oh, sweetheart. Don't worry, we will get there in time. But first, I need to ask an important question."

Zaharra moaned and arched her back, eyes fluttering closed as Kahr kissed the side of her neck, and bit her gently.

"Ask, ask anything, so long as it ends with you inside of me," she panted.

"Have you," Kahr asked, kissing his way down her neck, "ever lain with anyone before?"

He ended the question with a kiss to her lips as Zaharra fluttered her eyes open.

"What?" she whispered.

She could barely concentrate on the words he was saying over the roaring need flowing through her.

Kahr chuckled softly. "I just need to know. There is no wrong answer."

"Yes, a few times when I was a teenager. I was curious."

"And?"

Zaharra growled, getting slightly irritated. "And what? It was okay. It was nice. Are we done with the questions now?"

Kahr didn't answer, instead running his tongue up the side of her neck. He blew softly over the wet mark he made on her skin, the sensation something Zaharra had never felt before. A sensation that went straight to her core.

"All right, sweetheart. One last thing I feel like is important to discuss."

"Gods. What? If you keep stalling, I'm going to think you actually don't want to have sex with me," Zaharra growled.

He bit her earlobe, and all the irritation Zaharra felt about Kahr and his questions left her body instantly.

Everything he was doing felt really fucking good.

Kahr pulled back slightly, holding both of her wrists in one hand before sliding his free hand down her side to the bottom of her shirt.

His fingers skimmed over her skin between the hem of her shirt and the waistband of her trousers, and Zaharra whimpered at his touch.

"What?" she panted, as his fingers roamed slightly higher, grazing her ribs to the underside of her boobs. "What were you going to ask?"

Worship

Kahr kissed his way up Zaharra's neck while his free hand trailed over her overheated skin. He wanted her to whimper again, to moan again, to make all the noises and more. He wanted to tease her all night, but he had a feeling she wouldn't let him. At least not their first time together. She was just too impatient.

That was fine.

He planned on having her and touching her a lot more than just tonight.

"What?" she panted, as he trailed his fingers around to her lower back before pushing her hips up to grind into his. She whimpered again before continuing. "What were you going to ask?"

Kahr smiled and pulled back slightly, needing to see her expression for what he was about to say.

"Oh, I didn't have any more questions. I was just having fun irritating you."

Zaharra sucked in a sharp breath, narrowing her eyes at him. "You... you..." she growled before breaking his hold on her wrists. Unlocking her legs from around his waist, she bucked her hips, throwing them both over to the side. He landed on his back, Zaharra on top, and she forcefully placed her hands on his chest.

She scowled down at him. "You're not funny."

"I'm a little funny."

She rolled her eyes, grabbing the bottom of her shirt and pulling it off, throwing it to the side.

He sucked in a breath, letting his hands slide up her stomach to the edges of the thin wrap Zaharra wore around her breasts. He could feel the way her breath hitched as he sat up, pulling at the front laces to take off her covering. She threaded her hands through his hair as he dipped his head, licking and sucking at one of her nipples. Her low moan filled the air around them as he kissed his way across her chest to her other nipple, giving it just as much attention.

Her hands tugged at his head, her hips rolling and grinding against his. "Please. I need you. I really, really need..."

She trailed off as he dipped a hand into her waistband, fingers dipping down to find her clit.

Zaharra's strangled cry let him know when he hit the spot.

"Oh gods. Oh fuck." She tilted her hips up and into his hand.

"That's it, sweetheart," he murmured, and threaded his free hand through her hair, pulling her head back so he could kiss and suck on the underside of her neck.

Her cries turned sharp, more of a keening sound, and he knew she was close to coming. Kahr dipped a finger inside of her, still keeping the pressure on her clit. "Just like that, ride my hand. Come for me."

He pushed in a second finger, curling them forward. Zaharra gasped and shuddered, her pussy contracting on his fingers. She collapsed into him, mouth hungry for his as he continued stroking inside of her, prolonging her orgasm.

"Kahr, Kahr," she panted, kissing her way down his jaw to nuzzle her face into the side of his neck. "I, fuck, that feels so good. Don't stop, don't stop."

"Oh, sweetheart, I've only just begun."

He twisted them around, landing Zaharra back on the sleeping pad. She stared up at him, eyes glazed over from pleasure. He tugged at the laces at the front of his pants with his free hand, all while still keeping the rhythm with his fingers.

Zaharra bit her bottom lip, pushing at her own pants until she got them down her thighs. "Oh shit," she panted. "I still have my boots on."

Kahr couldn't stop the grin forming on his face as he continued pumping his fingers. She threw her head back and arched as he curled his fingers again, stroking the spot that had made her come earlier. "Fuck," she moaned, her hands gripping the sleeping pad. "Goddess, help me. I need you inside of me now."

"I am inside of you." He chuckled.

Zaharra's head snapped up, and she glared at him. "That is not what I meant, and you know it."

She gasped softly as he removed his fingers. He made sure she was watching as he put those two fingers in his mouth. Then he winked at her.

Zaharra's jaw went slack, her gaze intense as she watched him lick his fingers clean. A low, throaty sound erupted out of her, and she pushed at Kahr's chest, scooting out from under him as she reached for her boot laces.

"Off, off, off... get off," she chanted and threw a boot to the side before starting on the other one.

Kahr shook his head, having way too much fun with the effect he was having on her. He stood up, taking his time pulling off his own boots and stepping out of his pants. He waited as Zaharra stared up at him, her eyes lingering on his cock.

"Oh, it's... it's..." She reached out hesitantly, her fingers brushing gently across his shaft.

"Pierced?"

She glanced up, her eyes a little wide. "How many is that? Nine?"

Kahr nodded. "One for each inch, except for the head."

Her fingers ran down his shaft before she fully gripped him, and Kahr ground his jaw and closed his eyes. "Fuck, sweetheart. That feels good."

As she ran her hand up his shaft, he felt his cock involuntarily jerk, his knees going a little weak. It had been a while since anyone's hand besides his own had touched his cock.

He grabbed her hand, stopping her from going too far and making him come. Kahr knelt, pulling Zaharra under him. She let go of his cock with a sigh before hooking a leg over his hip and digging her nails into his back.

Settling in over her, he threaded his hand through her hair before kissing her long and hard. She arched into him as Kahr grabbed her thigh, lifting her higher up. He could feel the wet heat from her pussy against his cock, and he tightened his hold on her thigh. As Kahr moved his hips slightly, the tip of his cock teased her entrance.

She moaned, trying to move her hips, but Kahr held her in place. Breaking the kiss, he ran the tip of his tongue over her bottom lip. "Look at me, sweetheart."

The moment Zaharra opened her eyes, he pushed his hips forward, sinking the head of his cock into her. She gasped and whimpered as he stopped from going any farther. She sank her nails into his flesh. "Kahr, fuck. Please," she pleaded before throwing her head back as he pushed in another inch.

He tightened his fist in her hair. "Oh no, Zaharra. You are going to look at me the entire time, or else this is as much as you get."

Zaharra growled softly but met his gaze with her own. "I will kill you if you stop now."

Kahr smirked and slid in a few more inches.

"You're taking me so well, sweetheart." He tilted his head to kiss Zaharra's neck as her nails scraped up his back to grip his hair. Trailing light kisses across her jaw before reaching her lips, he pulled back, his lips hovering a hairsbreadth from hers. He locked his eyes with hers and finally gave her what she wanted, burying his cock fully inside of her.

Her sharp gasp was music to his ears as he released her thigh to smooth his hand up her side to her neck. Kahr wrapped his fingers around her throat lightly before he started rocking his hips.

The fire snapped and crackled, casting shadows across their skin as Kahr's breathing grew heavy, mingling with Zaharra's gasping moans. His lips met with hers as he felt her body shudder, her pussy contracting. "That's it, sweetheart. Come for me. Show me how much you enjoy my cock inside of you," he whispered before deepening the kiss and swallowing her sharp cries.

Kahr could feel himself lose control of his own slow thrusts, his hips jerking out of time as the pressure inside his cock swelled. He gripped both his hands in Zaharra's hair as he picked up the pace. The building pressure crested, causing all his muscles to tighten as he thrust inside of Zaharra as deep as he could, groaning gutturally as his cock jerked inside of her and they came at the same time.

Worth the Wait

Her eyes fluttered, barely able to keep them open, as Zaharra loosened her hands from the back of Kahr's neck and hair. Not a single word could describe what Zaharra was feeling. All she knew was that she didn't want to let go. She wanted to stay in this moment forever.

Kahr loosened his hands in her hair before pulling back, his nose rubbing against hers. She felt him move his hips, taking his time sliding out of her. He shifted to the side, gathering her in his arms to splay her boneless body over his.

She kissed his neck as his hands ran up and down her spine.

Shadows danced along the walls, the fire crackling in the background as Zaharra's eyes fluttered shut, her breathing heavy.

"Are you falling asleep, sweetheart?"

Kahr's deep voice elicited a shiver through her whole body, and Zaharra rubbed her face against the crook of his neck. "Mhhhh, no. Just resting my eyes."

Kahr's chest rumbled in silent laughter as she felt herself drift to sleep.

She woke with a start, hands clutching the soft fur over her naked body as she sat up. Zaharra blinked, slowly remembering that she wasn't at home. No, she was in the Midnight Mountains, in a cave, waiting out a storm with Kahr.

Her face grew heated as a dull ache pulsated between her legs.

She shook her head and glanced around, not really sure where the fur blanket covering her naked body had come from. The only thing that was the same was the bedroll she was lying on, plus the fire to her right. A high-pitched voice sounded from beyond the fire, deep within the shelter. Kahr's voice echoed out as Zaharra tucked her legs underneath herself to stand, wrapping the fur around her body.

She skirted the fire, heading towards the back of the shelter, where Kahr stood, his back towards her as he scrubbed at his arms, water sloshing slightly. He turned at her footsteps, a soft smile lighting up his face. "You're awake. I heated some water while you were asleep, if you wanted to clean up a little?"

"Where..." Zaharra trailed off, as a squeal sounded off to her right.

She turned towards the sound, surprised to see an opening, a dull glow barely illuminating the darkness beyond.

Ari zoomed out of the dim cavern, her wings careening her downwards into a spiral before she stopped, the force of air pushing strands of hair across Zaharra's face.

"Finally, you're awake. You should check out the rest of the shelter. It's so awesome."

Ari zoomed off, deeper into the dimly lit shadows, before Zaharra could say anything. Kahr gathered her in his arms, kissing her temple, and she leaned into him. "I thought she would be more vocal about what we did earlier."

"Oh, she was. You just slept through it."

Zaharra snorted, tilting her head up and kissing the side of Kahr's neck. "What did you say about cleaning up? Also, where did this come from?" She shrugged her shoulders against the fur blanket.

Kahr shifted his arms, turning her away from where Ari had disappeared. "Water, rags. It's not fancy, but it's what this shelter offers. And as for the fur..." he trailed off and kissed her temple. "I'll tell you after you explore the rest of the shelter."

Zaharra narrowed her eyes. "Better be worth the wait."

Kahr's arms tightened around her waist, and she nearly melted to the floor as he whispered in her ear. "Oh, I think it was totally worth the wait."

"That's... ohhh, you know that's not what I meant," Zaharra stammered, her face growing hot again.

"Hurry up!" Ari's yell traveled through the dim darkness, and Zaharra laughed.

"I don't think Ari is waiting around for me to clean up."

Kahr shrugged. "I'll distract her for a few minutes."

Zaharra bit her lower lip as she watched Kahr walk away, appreciating the view of his broad shoulders and muscular back. He was only wearing trousers, and it was a view she could get very used to. As he disappeared, she quickly dropped the fur and dipped a clean rag into the warm bowl of water, wiping herself down as fast as she could.

She wrapped her hair up into a messy bun on top of her head, using two of her smaller braids to keep it in place. Reaching for the fur, she stopped as she caught sight of Kahr's discarded shirt. She snagged it instead and tossed it on. It hit her mid-thigh, and she rolled up the edges of the sleeves.

Zaharra lifted her shoulder and turned her head, breathing in Kahr's scent of sandalwood and sweet spice. Her stomach fluttered and a soft smile settled on her lips before she turned and made her way deeper into the shelter.

The ground was hard-packed against her bare feet, the stone and dirt slightly warmer than she thought it would be. Lifting her hand, she trailed her fingertips across the grainy stone of the wall, and as she stepped into the second part of the shelter, her jaw went slack in awe.

Zaharra's eyes grew wide as she turned slowly in a full circle, taking in the glowing blue and green moss decorating the sides of the walls and large boulders. Taking a step closer, she hovered her fingers over the lightly glowing violet mushrooms growing from the cracks in the walls.

Where the moss and mushrooms didn't grow, art decorated the space. Handprints and smudges ranged in colors that varied between deep orange, yellowish, soft black, and some even a dark red. She followed the handprints as they went on and on until they faded into scenes of animals and people, big and small.

Stories decorated the cavern, and Zaharra's breath caught as she finally made her way over to Kahr. "What is this place?" she whispered.

He wrapped her in his arms. "Best I can guess, this place used to be a seasonal shelter when goliaths were more nomadic. Hundreds of years ago, before we started settling down in one place and building clans. Then later, it looks like we came back and used this place, in particular, for ceremonial practices worshipping the gods." He took a step back, pulling her along with him, and pointed to the ground. She knelt down, tracing the intricate designs carved into the rock floor. They were old and smooth, worn from the wear of time.

"I found this shelter, along with the caches filled with provisions like that fur blanket, when I was eighteen." Kahr continued. "I ended up living in this shelter for about three months after injuring myself."

Zaharra sucked in a breath and stood up, gently placing her hand on Kahr's chest. "How did you injure yourself? How bad was it?"

Kahr covered her hand with his own before bringing it to his lips and pulling her in close. "I'll admit, when I first came upon the ledge, I thought the same thing as you and braved the Ebon Hallow instead. I thought because I knew the mountains, and successfully traversed greater Ebon Hallow's before, that a small one would be easy. I ended up falling into a deep crevasse. Broke my ankle, and dislocated my knee, plus a mass of bruises and scrapes."

Zaharra shook her head. "That's... that's how you knew where to look to show me the shifting snow earlier? Was that where you fell?"

Kahr nodded.

She leaned into him, wrapping her arms around his waist. "I've only been injured once before. A few broken ribs, and it wasn't even from the training my mom put me through. It was because I fell out of a tree and landed on a vysha."

"I tore my wing once!" Ari pipped in from above them before floating down to Zaharra's shoulder. "A little over two years ago, on my sixteenth birthday. It got snagged on a sharp twig in a bird's nest after my friends dared me to steal an egg. Got into so much trouble with the parents because of it. I didn't even get the egg. Totally sucked. Anyway, I'm hungry. Is the moss edible?"

She jumped off of Zaharra's shoulder and floated down to a boulder, chopping off a small piece of glowing dark green moss with her little sword.

Before Zaharra could stop her, she put the moss in her mouth. Her face twisted in disgust, and she spit it out. "Uhggg. Gross. Tastes like dirt."

Kahr pinched the bridge of his nose and shook his head. "Ari. We have food in the packs. But if you really must eat something out of this cave, it's the mushrooms that are edible."

Zaharra covered her mouth with her hand to stifle a laugh as Ari stabbed one of the mushrooms and cut off a piece. She made the same face as before after taking a bite. "Still tastes like dirt."

Kahr sighed and slightly pushed Zaharra forward, back towards the front of the shelter. "Let's hurry and get Ari some real food before she decides to see what goliath and orc taste like."

By Your Side

ZAHARRA LOUNGED IN KAHR'S arms, watching the shadows dance along the stone walls while the fire snapped and popped merrily in front of them. Ari was fast asleep on a cozy bed she made on top of Kahr's pack, her little snores echoing through the shelter every few seconds.

Kahr's fingers played along her hip and upper thigh, drawing lazy swirls. "Do you think she is going to snorc all night?" he whispered in her ear.

Zaharra smiled. "Probably. But I'm sure we will get used to it until we get to your clan. Then she is definitely sleeping somewhere else."

Kahr's hand stopped, pressing heavily on her upper thigh, and Zaharra turned to look at him. His eyes had taken on a distant look, and she reached up to smooth the furrow between his brows. "What's wrong?"

"Nothing's wrong, sweetheart," he murmured before snaking her hand into his and kissing her palm. "It's just that I don't know if you really want to come to the summons with me."

This time Zaharra's brow furrowed. "You don't want me to come with you?"

"No, that's not..." Kahr shook his head. "I would never stop you from going anywhere with me. I honestly don't want to ever leave your side again. It's just that... How much do you know about goliaths and our culture?"

"Just the basics. Goliaths live in clans, mostly in the mountains, and very rarely leave. They are content staying outside of main society and live pretty basic life among nature."

Kahr took a deep breath. "Goliath clans are also pretty role dominated when it comes to the men and women. Many goliath men lean towards keeping the tradition of women as homemakers. Goliath women are not seen to be fighters or leaders. The culture is not as fluid and equal as orc culture is."

"Is that something you expect from me?" Zaharra asked, and Kahr shook his head.

"Gods no, sweetheart. Never change the way you are. There is a reason I left my clan and much of the goliath culture behind. I just don't want you to be shocked if you decide to come with me back to my clan."

She let out the breath she was holding. "Okay, good. For a moment there, I was worried. And it's already decided. You're not sending me back over that ledge without you."

Kahr smiled before squeezing her tighter to his side. "Well, I was going to suggest going down the western side of the mountain when we got to the crossover tomorrow. I would never send you back over that ledge without me."

"Good." She wiggled a little, getting comfortable. "Now that we know I'm coming with you, tell me what this summons is about and why you don't know how long it is going to take."

Kahr sucked in a deep breath. "It's about my family, my father specifically. I want to clarify that I was never close to him, and I never wanted to follow in his footsteps. He changed drastically after my mother left. Like I mentioned before, I basically raised my sister. By the time I turned eighteen, I couldn't spend another minute in his presence, and I left. Noreena wanted to stay. She still had faith in our father. I told her she was crazy. In the end, we left angry with each other. I told her it would take our father's death and a summons to make me come back up this damn mountain. So, that is what the summons is about. My father is dead."

"Oh, Kahr." Zaharra sighed and gave him a soft kiss before pulling away. "I don't know what to say except I'm here for you in any way you need."

"That's not all." Kahr sighed and turned away again, staring at the flickering flames.

"You don't have to tell me until you're ready."

He shook his head. "No, I do. It's the reason I don't know when I'll be returning. You need to know that my father was clan leader, and in goliath culture, clan leadership is lineage based. First, to the sons, then if the leader only has daughters, it will go to the eldest's husband if married, and so forth. I'm his first-born and only son, which means the clan is technically mine."

Zaharra sucked in a breath. "And it doesn't matter that you left? Your father dies and you just automatically become clan leader?"

Kahr nodded. "Unfortunately, yes, but I have no intention of leading the clan. There are ways for a leader to step down and appoint another. Our council has to approve of the successor if it's other than the current bloodline. But it can take some time, years even, which is why I didn't know how long I was going to be gone for."

Zaharra bit her lip as Ari's snores filled the sudden silence. She stared at the fire as she thought about what to say.

"Okay," she finally whispered. "Okay."

"Zaharra, you don't have to come with me. I should have—"

"No," she cut him off before rising to her knees and straddling his lap. Gripping his shoulders tight, she leaned her forehead onto his. His hands wrapped around her waist, pulling her into a tight embrace. "We are in this together. I mean that. I meant what I said before. When I am with you, it feels like home. And if we need to make this goliath clan our home for a little while, then so be it. I won't promise to behave like a good goliath woman, but I'll be by your side, stirring up trouble if you will have me."

Kahr tightened his embrace until she could barely breathe, his lips feather-light on hers as he tilted her chin up to kiss her. "Sweetheart, I wouldn't want you anywhere else. And please make trouble. It might just get us back down this mountain faster."

Zaharra kissed him back, running her hands up the back of his neck to tangle into his hair. Kahr loosened his hold and slid his hands down over her ass, to cup her thighs. She groaned as he deepened the kiss and flexed his hips at the same time.

She was still wearing his shirt and the thought that only the fabric between Kahr's hard, pierced cock and her pussy were his pants drove her slightly insane. Zaharra scraped her nails down his hard chest as Kahr ground his hips into her in a slow rhythm.

"Will you two be quiet? I'm trying to sleep."

Ari's irritated mutter washed over them, and Zaharra broke the kiss with a soft gasp. She had forgotten Ari was only a few feet away.

Kahr groaned and let his head fall back against the stone wall. "Shit. I forgot she was there."

"Me too." Zaharra sighed.

"She is right, though, sweetheart. We should get some sleep."

She slid off of Kahr's lap with a grumble, about to roll over onto her bedroll, when his hands gripped her hips. He dragged her into him, hard chest against her back.

"I said we needed to sleep, not that you had to run off and leave me cold and alone," Kahr whispered in her ear.

Zaharra smiled as he threw his leg over hers, pulling her in even tighter, before grabbing her hand and threading his fingers through hers.

"There we go, simply perfect. Now we can go to sleep."

She giggled before relaxing into his body, closing her eyes as the rhythm of Kahr's heartbeat lulled her to sleep.

No Turning Back Now

MORNING CAME QUICKLY, THEN night again. The second shelter they stayed in was barely an overhang with just enough room for them to lie under.

The night was clear as Zaharra rested, leaning against Kahr's side as they both stared up at the glittering stars. She pointed to the constellations she knew, and to her surprise, Kahr knew the stories behind each one.

That night, they fell asleep quickly, wrapped in each other's embrace.

As the second day came, they rose before dawn could catch them.

That morning started in silence. Even Ari was too tuckered out to make much of a fuss and rode on Zaharra's shoulder.

By mid-morning, the trail snaked downward, and by midafternoon, the ever-present snow and rocks gave way to a line of trees, seeming to appear out of nowhere on the horizon. Tendrils of smoke wove upwards, and the echoes of voices filtered through the air as they got closer.

Kahr stopped as they reached the tree line, his breath ragged.

His hand gripped hers tightly, and Zaharra leaned over to nudge his shoulder with hers. Her movement jostled the sleeping fairy, and Ari took to the air, hovering over the top of their heads.

"Oh, are we there?"

Kahr nodded, eyes trained forward.

"Ari, I want you to stay close. And be careful," Zaharra murmured.

"That's not a bad idea. I don't know what we are walking into. It's been over a decade since I last stepped foot here," Kahr said before swinging his gaze towards Zaharra. "I know you can handle yourself, but..."

"But even I know when to be quiet and observe. I know what I can handle and what I can't. I will not cause trouble until I know what's going on."

Kahr reached out to cup her face. "I guess there is no turning back now."

Zaharra pivoted slightly on her toes, pointing a finger over her shoulder. "Oh, we can definitely turn around and go home, but you and I both know neither of us will do that."

Kahr chuckled softly before pulling her into a hard embrace. She wrapped her arms around him just as fiercely.

"Enough waiting. Once we know what to expect, we can make a plan to get us back home sooner," Zaharra whispered before pulling back.

Kahr's arms lingered around her waist, his eyes flickering across her face. "All right, sweetheart. Let's go see how much of a mess we are walking into."

Zaharra headed down the well-worn trail twisting its way through the trees, Kahr by her side. As the sounds ahead grew louder, Kahr stepped closer to her side, hand resting on her lower back right below her travel pack. Her fingers tapped at her thigh, cataloging the weapons she had. Two.

The hatchet strapped to her pack and the small knife in her boot.

They would have to be enough for whatever situation they were walking into if it turned deadly.

No, that wasn't right.

She had more than two weapons.

Zaharra herself was a weapon.

Even if she wasn't destined to become a queen's guard, to follow in her family's legacy, Zaharra had still trained her whole life with the best.

It was time to put said training to the test.

"When we get to the clan, can I address the men directly, or must I go through you? Will they look to you if I do something unlady-goliath-like?" she whispered as they continued down the well-worn path.

"You can talk to anyone you want; you don't fall under our social norms. But the clan leaders and the married men will address me when talking to you. Unless something drastic has changed since I left," Kahr answered, the pressure of his fingers increasing on her lower back.

"You said I don't fall under the social norms. What rules must I follow?"

"Honestly, just don't kill anyone, and I think we will be fine, sweetheart."

Zaharra scoffed. "I'm not out here just chopping people's heads off for the fun of it."

They both grew silent as a goliath female stood along the path, a half-filled basket of white-gold berries in hand. She eyed Kahr cautiously, before staring openly at Zaharra. The woman pushed at the cradle strapped to her back, holding a sleeping infant.

Zaharra nodded slightly but kept moving, her pace steady as she continued down the path, passing a few more women and young children.

They were all in some state of gathering, from root plants to berries, some even prodding at the ground with sharp fire-hardened sticks. Every single one of them stared openly at Zaharra as she passed by.

They all dressed similarly, in long tunics and loose ankle-length skirts, varying in shades of earth tones. Coverings over their heads held back long dark hair. Their looks ranged from caution to bewilderment, but they never said a thing.

They stood as still as statues.

A shiver ran down her spine right before a young goliath boy, looking to be around eight years old, took off running on the path ahead of them, heading towards the village.

"Visitors! Visitors!" the child yelled.

"Well, I guess they know we are here." Zaharra chuckled, her laugh slightly cracking. She rubbed her sweaty palm on her thigh. "I'm a bit nervous," she whispered, as they strode out of the trees into a large clearing.

Kahr wrapped his arm around her waist, letting his fingers trail along her hipbone. "Me too, sweetheart, but everything will be fine, and like I said before, just be yourself."

"Right." Zaharra glanced around, taking in the scattering of wooden framed huts wrapped in weathered leathers and open fire pits. In the middle of the clearing, a larger hut stood, and the child made a beeline to a tall goliath woman with her back turned towards Kahr and Zaharra.

She was gesturing wildly at the three goliath men in front of her. The one in the middle stood a head taller than the rest, wearing a fur pelt over shoulders as wide as two tree trunks as he glared down at the woman. The goliath woman put her hand on his chest, as if to push him away, but the goliath man scowled even harder and grabbed her wrist. She twisted it in his grasp as he huffed and pushed her away. The poor woman stumbled back, but thankfully didn't fall.

Zaharra watched the woman's face harden, a fire burning bright in her eyes as she spit in the goliath's face.

Every sound in the small village seemed to pause, as if waiting for violence to erupt at any moment. The goliath man wiped at his face and reached out, grabbing the woman by her arm, dragging her forward.

"Oh, no you don't," Zaharra growled, having enough of whatever domestic dispute was happening right before her eyes. She sprinted forward without a second thought and slipped off her travel pack, throwing it at the towering goliath man in one movement.

The female goliath shifted out of the way as Zaharra's pack hit the goliath man in the face. The impact knocked him a step back, and her momentum carried Zaharra forward as she lowered her shoulder into the man's stomach, her arms wrapping around his legs to lift and slam him to the ground.

She followed him down, grasping his arm in her hands before flipping the gasping goliath man onto his stomach. Slamming one knee into the middle of his spine and the other on the back of his massive arm, she grabbed his braid and pulled his head back.

"Don't you know it's rude to pick on someone smaller than you?" Zaharra growled. "You should apologize."

The goliath struggled, but Zaharra had him pinned, and he wasn't going anywhere.

"How dare you attack a clan leader? Who do you think you are?" the goliath man spat. "What the fuck are you two doing? Get this wench off me."

Zaharra glared at the two goliath men who had been flanking the clan leader. They looked at each other before taking a hesitant step forward. Zaharra tightened her hold on the goliath man under her.

"Take another step forward, and I'll smash his face on the ground until he is unconscious. Then I'll do the same to the two of you."

The two men glanced at each other, and to Zaharra's surprise, the goliath woman stepped between them and knelt, pressing a small knife at the base of the goliath man's throat.

"Step closer and see what happens."

Zaharra's eyes widened as she met the woman's steely gaze. The rage she saw reflected in her eyes left no doubt in Zaharra's mind that the woman was fully capable of following through with her threat.

The Vote

ONE SECOND, ZAHARRA WAS by his side, and the next, she was flying across the clearing, tackling one of the biggest goliaths Kahr had ever seen in his life. He stood frozen, mouth agape as Zaharra easily flipped the man onto his stomach and pinned him to the ground.

"Wow," Ari breathed out in admiration as she floated in the air before him. "I want to learn how to fight like that."

"I want to marry that." Kahr sucked in a breath before shaking his head. He glanced at Ari, who was smirking at him. "Don't you dare tell Zaharra I just said that."

"Sureeee thing." Ari giggled before making a beeline towards Zaharra and the group of goliaths.

Kahr followed her closely, catching the tail end of the conversation.

"Step closer and see what happens."

Fuck, he needed to stop this now.

"Sister, stop!"

His shout echoed throughout the village, as its people watched the scene unfold in front of them.

If ice could burn, his sister's eyes would have set him on fire, as she slowly turned her head and set her sights on him.

A flicker of surprise seemed to show on her face, before her gaze turned icy once more.

"Oh, you must be Kahr's sister, Noreena," Zaharra said with a huge smile, still holding the massive goliath on the ground. "I'm Zaharra. It's so nice to meet you."

Kahr coughed slightly to cover up his chuckle as Noreena scowled at both of them.

To Kahr's relief, his sister removed her knife hovering at the goliath's throat.

"I'm surprised you came, Brother."

"It was a summons. I didn't have a choice."

Noreena scoffed before crossing her arms. "There is always a choice. But either way, you got here just in time."

"In time for what?"

"A vote," the goliath, still pinned under Zaharra, spat out and struggled some more. "Will you get your fucking wench to let go of me?"

Kahr eyed the goliath with a scowl. "Call her a wench one more time, and I'll let my sister make good on her threat."

"Oh my, oh my, what do we have here?" a new voice echoed out from behind Kahr, and he swiveled on his heel to see a line of five goliath men, all ranging in age, though they all had one thing in common. They all wore the fur pelts of clan leaders.

Just like the goliath under Zaharra did.

Fuck, what trouble did they just walk into?

The clan leader who spoke tilted his head, glancing around Kahr with a sigh. "Let Hunter up. We have pressing matters to attend to."

Kahr glanced over his shoulder and stared at his sister. "What do you want?"

His sister rolled her eyes before addressing Zaharra. "Release him."

Kahr took a step to the side as Zaharra released Hunter, shoving him into the ground to give herself the momentum to stand and take a few steps back. Kahr grabbed her by the waist, pulling her into his side. "Troublemaker," he whispered.

"Your sister doesn't seem happy to see you," she grumbled, eyes still trained on Hunter.

Hunter pushed himself to his feet, brushing the dirt from his clothes before wiping at his face. Blood trickled slightly from his lip, along with a few scrapes marring the left side of his cheek and chin.

He sized up Kahr slightly before shaking his head. "You need to talk some sense into your sister."

"Talk some sense... No, you don't get to dictate my life. Not anymore," Noreena growled, pointing at Hunter.

"Why doesn't everyone just take a breath and tell me what is going on?" Kahr asked.

"What is going on is that your sister has lost her mind. She wants to run the mountain."

Kahr stiffened, his hand tightening around Zaharra's waist as Noreena sneered.

"This isn't up to you. This is happening now that Kahr is here. I already know you don't approve, but I stopped caring what you thought about a long time ago."

"What is running the mountain?" Zaharra whispered as Hunter and Noreena continued to argue.

"It's an old tradition. Before leadership was heritage based, handed down from father to son, you proved your worth to lead by running the mountain. You are tested, and if the goddess Wylder finds you worthy, she blesses you. There hasn't been an active run in..."

"One hundred and sixty years."

Both Kahr and Zaharra spun to the side as the new voice, filled with steel and authority, startled them.

An older goliath woman, slumped from age, meandered past them, her walking cane hitting the ground with a hard thump every step forward.

"Enough from you two and your lovers' squabble. Is the hut set up for the ritual?"

"Not a lovers' squabble and you know that," Noreena muttered before grasping the front closer to the hut in front of her and pulling it open.

The older goliath woman tsked but didn't break her stride as she entered. Noreena followed quickly behind the woman, slamming the door shut. Hunter growled and followed, holding the door open for the other clan members who had been silent this entire time, leaving both Kahr and Zaharra behind.

"Soooo..." Zaharra began, "why were you summoned if your sister is just going to do this running-the-mountain tradition?"

"Because I'm next in line. There still has to be a vote. Someone has to step aside in clan leadership if she makes it through the trial and is blessed." Kahr sighed before rubbing at his face.

"This sounds like a good thing, though. You don't want to be a clan leader. Why do you look conflicted?"

"Because running the mountain is no easy feat. The tests can and have resulted in death before. Noreena wraps her stubbornness around her like a shield, but running the mountain is more than just physical. It is a spiritual journey. It is said when you travel to the goddess's realm, your very soul is on the line. If you die there, she gets to keep your soul, and even if you make it to her temple, and pass her tests, she could choose not to bless you."

Zaharra shivered as the magnitude of what Kahr's sister was trying to do sank in. "What are you going to do? Are you going to stop her?"

Kahr shook his head slightly before stepping forward to open the door. "I ... I don't know, but I guess we will find out together."

Her eyebrows shot up slightly. "You want me to go in there with you?"

Kahr smiled. "I always want you by my side, no matter what."

Ari floated down to Zaharra's shoulder. "Can I come too?"

"Of course, just be quiet and observe," Kahr murmured as Zaharra stepped past him and into the large hut.

He stepped in right behind her, shutting the door.

Kahr leaned against the door as the clan leaders stood in a row before the fire pit and a raised dais the older woman stood upon. Zaharra moved closer to his side, and out of the corner of his eye, he watched Ari zip up towards the long wooden beams spanning the entire ceiling.

Good, she would be safe and out of the way up there.

The fire in front of them burst to life as the elder goliath started to chant. A haunting melody filled the hut as the flames from the fire grew higher and higher. It spit sparks in their direction as the melody grew louder, and a few of the clan leaders flinched as the sparks hit their furs before sizzling out.

Kahr put his hand on Zaharra's lower back as the chanting came to a sudden halt and a feeling of otherness filled the silence. He could feel it weighing on his shoulders, pressing against his skin, and sucking the air from his lungs.

Zaharra tensed beside him, her breathing choppy.

The elder goliath on the dais raised her hands before slicing through the air, and just as suddenly as it came, the otherness was gone, and he could breathe. Zaharra inhaled deeply and swayed a little.

"What in the gods was that?" she asked.

Kahr leaned down and whispered, "She is an elder and a priestess who works heavy magic. It is said the elders can speak directly to the god or goddess they pray to."

The elder raised her eyes and scanned the room, lingering momentarily on Zaharra before moving on. Kahr swore her eyes glowed a light blue but couldn't be sure from all the shadow splaying off of the fire's flames.

"It has been one hundred and sixty years since the tradition of running the mountain has occurred.

A tradition in choosing clan leaders that has since fallen to the wayside. But a tradition, nonetheless, and a request that cannot be ignored. Once the rite begins, there is no turning back until you reach the goddess's temple or die trying."

The elder clapped her hands and threw a bundle into the fire, which erupted in a puff of thick smoke, a spicy fragrance lingering in the air. "Before we go any farther, we must take a vote. Clan leaders, step forward." The six men in fur pelts stepped forward, and Kahr blinked as the elder's gaze fell on him. "Come forward, Kahr. You are technically the leader of the Iron clan now, are you not?"

His stomach pitched, and he grimaced before stepping forward and away from Zaharra. Of course, he was technically the clan leader at the moment.

"Noreena, which clan leadership spot will you be running the mountain for?"

"Iron clan." His sister's voice rang out clearly.

He turned his head to look at her, but she wasn't looking at him, instead staring straight ahead, hands locked behind her back.

"Kahr, if your sister makes it back blessed by the goddess Wylder, will you step down as clan leader?"

Kahr glanced to his left, straight into the death glare of Hunter. The goliath in question shook his head slightly.

Fuck, he wished he had more time to think about this. "I would gladly hand over clan leadership to my sister without her running the mountain."

"And how would the other clan leaders vote for this? Would you allow Noreena to be clan leader without proving herself in the trial? She is technically blood-related."

"Women don't lead," Hunter growled, and three other clan leaders nodded.

"They can if blessed by the goddess herself," the older clan leader who had spoken up earlier snapped back.

Kahr narrowed his eyes slightly. He swore he knew him from his childhood, but his memory was coming up blank. But it seemed at least one clan leader was on his sister's side.

The remaining leader nodded. "We already voted. If your sister runs the mountain and returns blessed by the goddess Wylder, we will concede to her status as clan leader."

Kahr ground his teeth, his jaw popping.

So this really came down to him and his say.

Did he let his sister run the mountain and possibly die, or did he deny the request and lose his sister in another way entirely?

He glanced back towards Zaharra, his chest heavy with indecision. Her gaze locked onto his, telling him everything he needed to know. He had to let his sister go through with the trial. It was the only way. There was no stopping this.

Kahr nodded, before turning to face the elder.

"My sister will run the mountain."

"No!" Hunter shouted, moving forward.

The elder fixed Hunter with a withering stare, stopping him in his tracks, and Kahr felt the magic still lingering in the air thicken.

Hunter opened his mouth, but nothing emerged. Kahr watched the goliath man struggle, as if trying to move, his muscles bulging.

"You do not get to speak. The vote has been cast. Sit down," the elder commanded, and Kahr's eyes widened as the elders' magic shoved Hunter to the ground. Noreena snickered, and Kahr glanced her way with worry in his eyes. His sister met his stare, her face softening slightly before turning back to face the elder.

"Come, Noreena. To the dais quickly while the magic is at its peak."

"Wait." Kahr sucked in a breath, panic settling in his chest. "Are you sure you want to do this, Noreena?"

Fear laced his voice as his sister stepped onto the dais, lowering herself onto a freshly made bedroll. Another empty one lay next to her, and Kahr fixated on it. Why was there another bedroll?

"Brother, I have to do this. Don't worry too much while I'm gone. Just don't run my clan into the ground before I make it back."

"Why... Why is there another bedroll?" Kahr raised his voice.

Noreena crinkled her brow slightly and glanced up at the elder. "Why *is* there another bedroll?"

The elder glanced around the room, her gaze landing behind Kahr. "Because someone is coming with you."

Kahr stiffened as Zaharra stepped to his side, the tips of her fingers grazing his arm.

"What do you mean?" Both Kahr and Noreena spoke at the same time.

The elder ignored them both as she reached her hand towards Zaharra, and Kahr felt his entire world sway at her next words.

"The goddess Wylder is interested in you, Zaharra Fairstone."

Magic Calls

Zaharra's eyes locked with the elder's.

She had felt the magic. A calling she couldn't explain, but she knew somehow she would be running the mountain alongside Kahr's sister.

Her grip tightened on Kahr's forearm, gaze flickering to his face.

She could see the turmoil playing out over his features. "Kahr," she whispered as he reached out to cup her face.

She wanted to tell him it would be alright, that she knew what she was doing, but the truth was she didn't know. She truly didn't know if this would be the last time she would see him.

So, she said the only thing she knew to be the truth.

"I need to do this too."

His eyes searched her face before he sighed and rested his forehead against hers.

"You will come back to me. You and my sister, both of you."

Zaharra lifted her chin, brushing her lips against his, before pulling away and taking the elder's hand.

She settled in on the bedroll next to Noreena before glancing her way.

Kahr's sister had a peculiar look on her face that Zaharra couldn't place. She offered her a shrug, trying to make light of the situation looming before the both of them. "Girl-on-girl bonding time?" She cracked a joke before the elder cleared her throat and raised her hands above them, chanting in a language Zaharra could only describe as ancient.

As if the land itself spoke.

She could hear the wind blowing through flowered meadows, water crashing on a rocky shoreline. The crumbling of rocks sliding down a mountain's side and the soft fall of snow floating through the air.

The elder knelt and thrust her hands into the fire before standing again, raining ashes down over the both of them.

If the air felt heavy before, it was now suffocating.

She couldn't breathe.

She couldn't move.

It felt like she was standing still and falling all at the same time as darkness swallowed her whole.

Zaharra came to with a sharp breath, eyes snapping open. Clear blue skies greeted her as the sound of birds cried out in the distance. She sat up cautiously and looked around.

She was in the middle of a forest, fallen tree leaves and needles prickling at her palms. Noreena lay on her side, eyes closed. Her chest rising and falling in a steady rhythm.

Zaharra got to her feet in silence, slowly spinning in a circle to take in their surroundings.

To their left, the trees parted, as if hinting at a trail beyond. A few boulders lay that way, along with a small travel pack.

"Fuck, that was an... experience," Noreena's groggy voice echoed out, and Zaharra glanced over her shoulder as the goliath woman pushed herself off the ground and brushed a few stray leaves from her hair.

"My thoughts exactly," Zaharra muttered. "Where are we?"

Noreena took a deep breath and glanced around with a frown. "A forest."

"Well, yes. I figured that out already, but do you know where?"

Noreena sighed and pinched the bridge of her nose. "How much do you know about running the mountain? And the trial? Also, are you nauseous, or is it just me?"

"A little, but it's wearing off. And nothing, really. Back at the hut was the first I heard of it."

Noreena glanced at Zaharra, surprise clear as day across her face. "Seriously? You just agreed to go based on... nothing? You just thought, let's go have some fun traversing a spiritual realm?"

"Is that where we are? A spiritual realm?"

Noreena dropped her hand and stared at Zaharra.

She shrugged in return. "It just ... felt like the right thing to do. I figured you would explain everything later."

Noreena opened her mouth before snapping it shut and shaking her head. Taking a deep breath, she rubbed at her face. "Alright, so you know nothing about the trial and running the mountain."

"Kahr said that it's a test from the goddess Wylder to see if you are fit to lead. And in the hut, you heard the elder. The goddess wanted to meet me. What was I supposed to do, tell the elder and in turn, the goddess, no?"

"Few do."

The small voice echoed out from behind Zaharra, and she spun on her heel, putting herself in front of Noreena. She pulled the small knife out of her boot, holding it out in front of her. "Who said that?"

"More like... what," Noreena whispered, leaning into Zaharra and pointing over her shoulder. "I think it came from the lymer."

Zaharra narrowed her eyes at the lymer in question, sitting on the boulder with its bushy tail in hand. It picked at a bur before tossing it in their direction.

"Well, I know who is the smarts in this duo," the lymer squeaked.

"Rude," Zaharra murmured. "Sorry if I didn't expect talking animals in this place."

Noreena moved out from behind Zaharra, and she shot her arm out to hold the goliath back.

"It's fine. It's just a lymer," Noreena whispered.

"Is it, though? Talking animals doesn't scream caution? Proceed carefully?"

"Funny. I like you. But the goliath is right. I'm just a lymer, and I'm here to give you a message from the goddess."

"Ohhhh, just like in the stories. This is exciting." Noreena grasped Zaharra's shoulders and shook her slightly.

"All right," Zaharra sighed, though she kept her knife held outright. She wasn't going to trust the talking lymer just because it said so.

The lymer cleared its throat slightly before standing on its hind legs, projecting its squeaky voice. "Welcome to the goddess Wylder's realm. While your bodies lie in the mortal realm, the goddess's magic will nourish you. You will not hunger or thirst, but if you break or bleed in her realm, your bodies back home will also bear the same marks. The goddess is giving you three days to find her temple. Along the way, you will be tested. If you do not find Wylder's temple in the time allowed, she will send you back unblessed. Not only that, but she will strip your family line from ever being able to lead again. Good luck and try not to die."

The lymer launched itself onto the nearest tree, disappearing within seconds.

Zaharra gulped and lowered her knife.

"Still excited for the talking lymer?" she asked as she felt Noreena's grip on her shoulders tighten.

"Yes. I love talking animals."

Zaharra turned her head, eyeing Kahr's sister. "Are you feeling okay? Don't take this the wrong way, but back at the village you seemed more... reserved."

The goliath grinned, hugging Zaharra tightly from behind. "I'm feeling fantastic. Aren't you? I'm super excited to bond with my brother's girl."

"Right, Noreena, did you eat something since getting here? Or touch anything..."

She trailed off as Kahr's sister started swaying slightly and released her hug, leaving dusty smudges on the front of Zaharra's shirt.

She hissed quietly through gritted teeth. Noreena had definitely touched something.

Zaharra glanced around, trying to find anything that would have transferred dust onto the goliath. She padded slowly over to where Noreena had woken up and cursed under her breath. Squatting carefully, she touched a few crushed flowers with her knife. The petals shook slightly, dusting the steel of her knife in an off-white pollen.

Noreena must have crushed them somehow...

Shit, she had rubbed her face while talking, most likely inhaling the dust.

"Noreena, did you touch anything else?" she called out before glancing behind her.

Anxiety burst through her veins, rocketing through her whole body as she stood up and spun in a circle.

"Noreena!" Zaharra yelled again, knowing she had epically fucked up.

She knew something was messing with Noreena's state of mind and she just let her out of her sight.

And now she was gone.

Have Faith

HE COULD HEAR THE distant murmur of the clan leaders behind him, but he didn't care. The only thing he could focus on was the swell of magic and how the two most precious women in his life had gone deathly still.

The elder shook her hands before clapping the soot from them. "Well then, off with you all. You will be informed if they make it back."

Kahr jerked slightly. "They will make it back. They have too."

The elder looked at him, eyes seeming to bore right through him. "I see, in your heart, you believe this. It is good for you to have faith. But you have a job to do now, do you not?"

Kahr shook his head. "What?"

"We didn't summon you here just to sit and watch over your sister during the trial. You have a clan to run."

Kahr narrowed his eyes and crossed his arms. "And what if I want to sit here and watch them? I am the clan leader, am I not?"

A hand landed on his shoulder, startling Kahr. He turned quickly, coming face to face with the one clan leader who had been on Noreena's side.

"Have faith, like the elder said, but she is right. Run the clan while your sister fights for her place to stand with us. We don't want her to be returning to chaos when she gets back."

Kahr clenched his jaw, looking down at his sister before his gaze traveled to Zaharra. "I can't."

The clan leader gripped his shoulder tightly. "You can. You always could, even when you shouldn't have had to."

His eyebrows knitted together before turning and staring long and hard at the clan leader. "How do I know you?"

The clan leader tilted his head before he cracked a smile. "Well, I deserve that. You haven't seen me since your mother left."

Kahr closed his eyes with a sigh, his memories finally putting two and two together. "Thoreston. It's been... It's been over twenty-five years."

The clan leader nodded. "Yes, well. I am not proud of how I left. And then some unpleasantness happened with my clan and family that I had to deal with. When I finally had the courage to come back, you had already left. Your father... Well, he had changed immensely, and your sister never really knew who I was to begin with."

Kahr shrugged Thoreston's hand from his shoulder. "Thanks for supporting Noreena today, but I think all the clan leaders should leave, you included. I'll be fine here on my own."

To his credit, Thoreston took a step back, hands raised slightly. "If you change your mind. You know where to find me. I would truly love to catch up."

He nodded as Thoreston and the rest of the clan leaders made their way out of the hut. Hunter's cold-blooded stare didn't go unnoticed by Kahr as he left last, slamming the door on his way out.

Kahr's jaw ticked, his shoulders tight as he stared at the closed door. The clan would be fine without him for a fucking night.

He glanced at the elder, who had gone silent after his interaction with Thoreston. She sat next to the fire and whittled at a chunk of wood in her hand, feeding the shavings to the flames.

He silently took a seat next to Zaharra and trailed his fingers softly across her cheek. A slight buzzing of wings had him glancing up towards the wooden beams, and he raised his hand towards Ari as she floated down.

"Not going to lie, but I forgot about you. How are you holding up?"

He expected the little fairy to scoff or stick her tongue out at him. But she did neither, instead hopping out of his hand to land on his knee and sit down, her focus entirely on Zaharra and Noreena.

"How long until they wake back up?" Ari whispered.

"When they finish running the mountain," the elder answered as she continued to whittle. "And before you ask, Kahr, it is just like in the stories you were told as young children. Their spirits will run through the goddess's realm and she will test them. Their mortal bodies will not need food or water during this time, but whatever injuries they sustained in Wylder's realm will show upon their mortal bodies."

"Why did the goddess want Zaharra to go?" Ari asked.

The elder chuckled softly. "Because the goddess is curious about your orc. She wants to test her."

"She doesn't deserve to be tested this way," Kahr growled. "She was just getting over..."

He trailed off as the elder turned her head to stare at him.

"Getting over... Oh my, stupid boy. One does not just get over being part of the Fairstone bloodline. Yes, the goddess knows who your lover is, and by her grace, so do I. Do you even know her family history? Zaharra is right where the fates need her to be. Change is in the air for goliath kind, and your sister will be the one to implement it. And she will not fail as long as a Fairstone is by her side."

Ari lifted off Kahr's knee, wings buzzing aggressively. "Don't call him stupid. Zaharra is the only one who gets to call him that, you old bat."

"Ari!" Kahr reached out to grab the angry fairy from the air. "Apologize to the elder right now."

"No, just because you're old doesn't give you the right to be mean and you don't get to tell me what to do. I'm eighteen and an adult, damn it."

The elder chuckled and motioned for Kahr to release Ari. "Oh, I like your spirit, young one. Come, come join me by the fire. I want to know more about you."

"I can't believe I have to say this to you as well, but play nice," Kahr murmured before releasing Ari. He watched as she buzzed over to the elder, making sure she wasn't about to do anything stupid.

He took a deep breath as Ari settled in on the elder's shoulder, their voices low as they started speaking to each other.

"Wait," he growled softly. "When did Zaharra call me stupid? Ari, when did Zaharra call me stupid?" he asked a little louder.

Ari waved her hand at him in a shooing motion. "When she came running after you up the mountain. She called you many things. Now be quiet. The elder is telling me a story, and you are interrupting."

Kahr snorted and shook his head, his gaze going back to Zaharra. He pushed a strand of her hair out of her face and behind her ear. "Can you please hurry back? I'm not sure how long I can take being bullied by a teenaged fairy. She was your stray you picked up. Can't believe you just flounced away and left her with me while you went on some epic quest with my sister. And you..." He leaned over to straighten the ties on his sister's tunic. "I hope you aren't being to mean to my..."

Kahr paused.

Calling Zaharra his girlfriend didn't seem right. She was so much more to him than that. He knew from the moment Zaharra entered his life that she was the one. The other half of his soul.

"I hope you are getting along with the love of my life, Noreena. I know Zaharra can take care of herself, but she still needs someone to look out for her. Don't push her away because if I know my woman, she will make sure you make it through the trial, no matter what. But I need you to be the leader I know you will be and make sure Zaharra comes home with you."

The slight creaking of the hut door drew Kahr's attention, and he stood as a small goliath woman snuck in. She skirted around the fire, headed towards the dais before pulling up short.

"Oh, I ... I didn't..." the goliath woman stuttered before glancing to the ground. "I didn't realize anyone but the elder would still be in here."

Kahr gave the woman a hard look. "Who are you, and why are you here?"

The goliath woman peeked up with one eye, her shoulder-length dark hair covering the entirety of her left face. Her gaze shifted, landing on Noreena, then Zaharra. She bit her lip and scrunched the one eyebrow Kahr could see. "So it's true. There is an orc woman here."

Kahr stepped off the dais, cutting off the goliath woman's view of Zaharra and Noreena. He didn't want anyone gawking at them.

The one eye he could see widened before she bowed her head. "I'm sorry. I just..." She gulped before lifting her head and took a deep breath.

"Noreena is running the mountain for me."

Running the Mountain

"DAMN IT. GET BACK here. Noreena!"

Zaharra yelled for Kahr's sister again as she made her way through the thick forest. She nicked the closest tree trunk with her knife, marking her path before squatting down and pressing her hand against the ground. She was pretty sure Noreena had gone this way, but something just felt off about this forest.

Normally, Zaharra had no issue tracking, and a goliath high on whatever dust that flower produced would leave a pretty decent trail behind.

And yet...

Zaharra shook her head and glanced behind her. She couldn't even see the trail she was making. It was almost as if the forest was eating away any traces of her footsteps left behind.

A loud giggle floated on the wind, and Zaharra shot up, turning towards it.

"Noreena! Just stay where you are."

She crashed through the low underbrush, following the giggle. Relief flowed through her body, replacing her growing anxiety as she caught sight of Noreena.

She was attempting to climb a tree, something high up in the branches catching her attention.

Zaharra lengthened her stride before crashing to a halt in front of the overly joyous goliath woman. "Damn it, Noreena, I need you to stay by my side until this shit wears off. At which..."

Shushing her, Noreena pointed up. Her grin was still plastered to her face. "Look, look. Look at the babies."

"Right, babies. Just stay put for a moment," Zaharra murmured without looking up. She shrugged the travel pack that had been left next to the boulder off her shoulder before rifling through it. She hadn't had time to go through the pack before running after Noreena, but she hoped there was something inside that would keep the goliath attached to her side until the flower's dust wore off.

"Rope, yes." Zaharra said as she pulled out a considerable length of rope from the pack.

Zaharra made quick work, wrapping the rope around her shoulders and chest, before doing the same to Noreena. She took a step back to admire her handiwork before grabbing the travel pack and slinging it over her shoulder again.

"Right, now you aren't getting away."

Noreena didn't pay her any mind, still staring up at the tree branches and wiggling her fingers. She made little kissy sounds.

Zaharra glanced up and sucked in a sharp breath. Fuck.

Yellow glowing eyes stared down at them, mouths bared to show sharp little teeth. Claws gripped the tree limbs with paws half the size of Zaharra's hands.

Baby mountain leopards.

And where there were babies, a mother would be nearby.

A low growl echoed through the forest, and Zaharra held her breath as she slowly turned.

Just her luck. Mama had found them.

The snow leopard was huge, with paws as big as Zaharra's head. It bared finger-sized fangs as it prowled closer. Its glowing eyes locked with hers, and Zaharra took a small step back, nudging Noreena with her body.

"Ohhh, big kitty looks mad," Noreena whispered.

"Big kitty is mad. Let's get away from its kits before she gets furious," Zaharra whispered back.

"I want to pet it."

Zaharra cursed and grabbed the goliath's arms, tucking them behind her, holding her in place as the snow leopard hissed at the sudden movement. Its saliva landed on her bare forearm, and Zaharra flinched as it burned and blistered her skin.

Of course, every animal in this place had to be special. Talking lymers and fire-spitting leopards. She really didn't want to imagine what could be next.

Noreena hissed back at the leopard before giggling. "Let me pet the kitty."

Zaharra shook her head and pulled Noreena back with her, a few small steps at a time. The goliath woman was strong, though, and it was beginning to be a struggle to keep her in place.

She needed to come up with a plan, and fast, because the look in the snow leopard's eyes was one that didn't need any explanation.

It wanted to kill them both.

"Kitty, kitty, kitty."

Zaharra slapped her hand over Noreena's mouth as her mind filtered through her limited possibilities.

They could either fight or run.

And Zaharra refused to fight the leopard who was only protecting her kits.

Which left them with running...

Except where could they run to?

She pushed them both back another step, her mind racing through different scenarios as the snow leopard advanced.

Then she heard it.

The sound of rushing water.

An idea blossomed in her mind, and Zaharra bent down slowly, picking up a rock. She threw it at the leopard and turned, tossing Noreena over her shoulder before sprinting with every ounce of energy she had.

She didn't know if the leopard gave chase.

She didn't know if at any second they would be taken to the ground.

The only thing she did know was the trees were thinning and the sound of the water was growing louder by the second.

The drop-off appeared out of nowhere, the thrashing and foaming river only a few feet below.

She didn't hesitate as her feet left the ground, and Noreena screamed as the water enveloped them both.

Any air Zaharra still had in her lungs evaporated as the freezing river rushed over her head, ripping Noreena from her shoulder and whipping them both back and forth. Her feet hit the rocky bottom of the river only to be swept out from under her as the rope tying her to Noreena pulled taut.

Zaharra thrashed, trying to swim to the surface while the current dragged her downriver. She slammed against a huge rock, pain lancing up her spine and neck, and her lungs screamed for air. An arm wrapped around her chest, and her head broke the surface, gasping in sweet relief.

"Hold on! I've got you," Noreena yelled as the current tried to take them both under again.

Zaharra sputtered slightly as water splashed over her head, but somehow Noreena managed to keep them both afloat, swimming with the current while still angling towards the opposite side of the river.

Shivers racked her body as Noreena pulled herself up the embankment and out of the river. She reached down and Zaharra clasped her hand in hers. Kahr's sister hauled her out of the water, and she landed with a wet thud, face down, coughing and struggling to get enough air into her lungs.

"It's going to be okay. We are going to be okay," Noreena yelled over the sound of the river, all while patting Zaharra's back.

She turned her head to get a good look at the goliath. A small cut snaked its way across her forehead, the blood a watery pink running down over her eyebrow. "You're hurt," Zaharra rasped.

Noreena shook her head and pressed at the cut. "I'm fine. Thanks to you. I don't know what happened back there. Only that, one moment I was thinking clearly, and then...I was just..."

"Overly joyous and obsessed with frolicking through the woods."

Noreena shook her head, a grimace settling across her lips, as more shivers rocked through

Zaharra. "It's getting dark. We need to find shelter and build a fire. It would be a shame to die from the cold after everything we just went through."

"For once, we agree." Zaharra groaned as Noreena helped her to her feet. Her back smarted, and it hurt to take a full breath, but they were both still alive.

Noreena gathered up the excess rope between the harnesses holding them together. "The rope harness was a smart idea."

"Thanks," Zaharra mumbled as her teeth began to chatter. "You were being a pain and running away from me."

The goliath woman snorted before shaking her head. "Let's get going before the temperature drops. I have an idea or two about where we might find some shelter for the night."

The Healer

"WHAT DO YOU MEAN, she is running the mountain because of you?" Kahr asked.

The goliath woman bit her lip. "It's complicated, but long story short, we... Noreena and I are in a relationship."

Kahr narrowed his eyes. "You sure you aren't being delusional, because the last thing I want to deal with is another goliath thinking they are in a relationship with my sister when they clearly aren't."

The goliath woman's mouth turned down at the corners. "You're talking about Hunter. He is an asshole and is not fit to be a clan leader. Nor are they in a relationship anymore. Haven't been for some time."

"You can trust her. She doesn't lie," the elder called out as she added another log to the low-burning fire.

"I'm Orina. And..." The goliath woman turned to motion towards the elder. "Mervian is my great grandmother. But I'm sure that means nothing in ways of convincing you Noreena and I are in a relationship, does it?"

Kahr shook his head. "Sorry, but after what I witnessed earlier, I'm just a little suspicious of, well...everything and everyone."

"As well you should be." Orina spoke softly before sitting down at the edge of the dais. "I would expect no less from Noreena's big brother, always the protector. She told me stories about when you two were younger." Glancing at his sister, she sighed. "I just want to be here for her. Please don't make me leave. Even if you don't believe me."

Kahr sighed, pinching the bridge of his nose. "Fine. Stay. But the moment I step out of this hut, you do, too. No one but Ari and the elder are allowed in this hut without me."

Orina nodded. "Of course, thank you. Who is Ari?"

"That's me!" Ari shot up off the elder's knee and floated through the air.

Orina's face lit up. "Oh, my goddess! All this talk about running the mountain, Noreena's brother being back, and an orc woman being in the village and no one mentioned a fairy. It's such a pleasure to meet you, Ari."

Ari buzzed around Orina's head a few times before landing next to her. "So you're Noreena's girlfriend? Why does she need to run the mountain because of that, and what about that big goliath earlier? The one Zaharra beat up?"

Kahr sat down next to Zaharra, watching as Orina and Ari started talking. He didn't want to admit it, but their voices filling the silence gave him a sense of relief. Something else to focus on besides the worry growing inside of him.

"Goliath culture is ... different. We are trying to change some things, and Noreena is convinced if she runs the mountain, it will be easier to sway the clan leaders to our ideas. I told her it didn't matter, all that mattered was the clan and what they thought. All that matters is that I believe in her. The clan already sees her as their leader. But my Noreena is stubborn, and she is convinced she needs the goddess's blessing to be a good leader, and to be worthy of me. And as far as Hunter goes, we all have mistakes in our past. Hunter is one of Noreena's. Though, to be fair, he was great at hiding who he truly was in the beginning. He showed his true colors though when her father got sick."

Orina glanced in Kahr's direction. "A cut got infected. Then he got sick with a cold that worsened and got into his lungs. Over the years, any minor cold or injury progressed into something more. His body just refused to get back into fighting shape. Not sure if anyone actually told you how he passed."

Kahr shook his head and glanced towards the fire. "I just assumed it had something to do with his drinking."

"He stopped drinking ten years ago. When Noreena threatened to leave, just like you did."

"She threatened to leave?"

"She did. He changed his ways, or at least that is what Noreena told me. I never knew your father the way you two did. I was just the one who helped take care of him in his final years. It's how Noreena and I met."

Kahr tightened his jaw, his chest aching slightly. His eyes burned as he continued staring at the fire. "I'm glad he changed and my sister could see him differently. Are you a healer, then? You said you took care of our father in his final years?"

He needed to change the subject. Talking about his father was proving to be a little more difficult than he expected it to be.

"I'm a healer, yes, though many of the people I care for are those who are nearing the end. The god Ebon and I have a bit of a special relationship."

"What type of relationship?" Ari asked. "Ohhh..."

On Ari's sharp exclamation, Kahr turned to look in Orina's direction. She had pulled her hair from the side of her face she was hiding. Deep scarring ran over the side of her face, starting at her scalp and snaking its way down to her lips. Her eye was a milky white as she turned to catch Kahr's stare.

"There is more scarring on my arms, stomach, and thighs. An ice bear mauled me when I was younger. I was found two days later by Gran Gran, isn't that right?"

Mervian sighed and held up the wooden carving she had been working on. To Kahr's surprise, it was a small rendition of a bear. His eyebrows shot up to his hairline as the elder tossed the finished carving into the fire. "You are blessed by Ebon himself. Still don't know why you turned to healing instead of becoming a priestess."

Orina chuckled as her great grandmother pulled out another piece of wood and started carving.

"She likes to sacrifice the bear statues to the fire to thank Ebon for not taking me. Been doing it for years. Personally, I'm over what happened, but everyone processes their emotions in different ways."

"I don't know how I would process if anything happened to Zaharra," Kahr whispered. He glanced over his shoulder, his eyes taking in the two still bodies behind him. "Even now, I can't bear the thought of walking out of that door and trying to run the clan. I know logically I can't help them in the goddess's realm, but I feel like... I don't know, it's stupid."

"Like your presence can mean the difference in the outcome. That if you take your eyes off them for just one second, something bad could happen? It's not stupid. It's called being in love."

Kahr nodded and rubbed the palms of his hands against his eyes. "It's just... I just, I need to stay here tonight at least. The clan can run itself for the night, right?

Orina nodded. "I think the clan will be fine until the morning."

Kahr's brow furrowed slightly, and he got up, moving closer to his sister and Zaharra. "Orina," he whispered, "Get over here."

Dropping to his knees, he wiped at the slow-bleeding cut that appeared out of nowhere on Noreena's forehead. She was cold, frighteningly so, and Kahr put the back of his hand on Zaharra's forehead. She was the same.

"Fuck. Fuck. Fuck," Kahr chanted as fear spread throughout his body. "What is happening to them over there?"

Orina fell to her knees by his side and grabbed his hand in hers. "It's going to be okay. It has to be. They will make it back."

Kahr clenched his jaw as he sat there, his hand still pressed to Zaharra's deathly cold skin. "Is there anything we can do? A way to warm them up?"

"No," Orina whispered, her voice cracking. "All we can do is sit here and pray."

He shook his head and released Orina's hand. "No. I'm not just going to sit here and pray. Fuck that." Kahr moved and gathered Zaharra's dead weight in his arms, wrapping his body over hers. "You will not die. You hear me, sweetheart." He pressed his face into the crook of her neck, shivering slightly. "Take my warmth. Take whatever you need from me. Just make it back home."

Out of the corner of his eye, Kahr saw that Orina had snuggled up behind his sister, wrapping her arms around her. "Baby, if you can feel me, know that I am there with you. I won't leave you."

Kahr closed his eyes, and pulled Zaharra closer. His lips moved in silence praying to any, and all, who would listen. To any god or goddess who would bring his love back to him alive.

The Goddess's Realm

"How did you know there was going to be a shelter here?" Zaharra shivered, her teeth chattering as she held her hands out in front of her.

Noreena pressed up against her side, shivering in sync with her.

Their little fire barely put a dent in the cold she was feeling, but at least it was something.

What was really helping, though, was the small cave Noreena found just as night fell.

"I noticed something earlier, even though I was out of my mind." Noreena chattered as she squeezed even tighter into Zaharra's side. "The forest seemed so familiar, and then the river. Finding the shelter solidified my hunch."

"Which was?" Zaharra wrapped her arms around Noreena's shoulders and scooted a little closer to the fire. Her bare toes hovered over the line of almost being in the fire, but she didn't care. If they did catch on fire, then at least she would be warm, right?

"The midnight mountains and the land in the goddess's realm mirror each other. Which means, I know where we are." Noreena wrapped her arms around Zaharra the same way she had them around her. "All we have to do is not freeze to death, and I can get us to the goddess's temple before our time runs out."

"Oh, is that all?" Zaharra laughed as she watched her breath mingle with the cold air. "Let me just put my whole body into this tiny little fire of ours to warm up, then we can be on our way."

Noreena snorted, following up the noise with a full-body shiver. "Not if I throw my body into the fire first. I think I have dibs, considering it was you who plunged us headfirst into the river and I had to save us from drowning."

"Says the goliath who wanted to pet the mountain leopard with a mouth full of fire." Zaharra huffed and flexed her hand in memory. There was a small blister on her forearm where the mountain leopard's saliva had hit her, but thankfully it didn't hurt. Not in comparison to the lingering pain in her lower back and ribs.

"I still can't believe right from the start I fucked up so badly," Noreena whispered.

"You? No, I was the one who knew you were acting odd, and I let you out of my sight. I was the one who fucked up right from the start."

Noreena sighed and shifted, pushing her feet as close to the fire as they could get. "Do you think our boots and socks are dry yet?"

"Maybe, but I don't want to move yet. My toes are finally warm. And I've also come to realize something."

"What?" Noreena whispered.

"I really, really despise being cold."

Noreena's laugh echoed through the tiny shelter, and Zaharra laughed right alongside her. Her thoughts went to Kahr as they shivered next to the fire, their laughter falling away as the small cave filled with the sound of silence.

"What do you think Kahr is doing right now?" She whispered.

Noreena shrugged. "I don't know. Hopefully leading the clan. I hope Orina introduced herself."

"Orina? Who is Orina?" Zaharra asked before slowly loosening her hold on Noreena with a groan. Her back was getting stiffer by the minute, and she knew eventually she would have to get up and stretch. But at this moment, all she really cared about was checking on their socks, which they had laying on a large rock next to the fire. She rotated them around. They were still a little damp but drying off quicker than she expected.

She checked their boots next. They were already dry, only the fur on the top parts still being wet.

"Orina is my fiancée. Or at least she will be once I get back and propose to her the moment I open my eyes. How are the socks?"

Zaharra shook her head and fed bits of old bark and twigs into the fire. "You are really going to ask about our socks right after telling me you have a fiancée? Or almost fiancée. I thought that big goliath and you were a thing."

"If by thing you mean a past mistake, then yes. But if we are going to be talking about love lives, we should talk about you and my brother. How long has that been going on for?"

Zaharra smiled and felt her cheeks heat slightly, even though she was still freezing. "It's... Well... I want to say still new, but we met a few months ago after I got home. We actually..." She snorted. "I actually threw him on his ass the first time we met. Then I made him give me a job."

Noreena laughed. "That is impressive. What does my brother do for a living?"

"Oh, you don't know? He is a trader. He has a shop in the village. Though technically not anymore, because he gifted it to me..." Zaharra trailed off as Kahr's sister stared at her with wide eyes, and a shocked expression filling her face.

"I feel like there is a lot you are leaving out. You should start at the beginning."

Zaharra opened her mouth before snapping it shut. The beginning... The beginning would mean talking about how she failed at the one thing she had trained her whole life to be, a queen's guard.

"What is it? Your expression changed." Noreena asked.

She shook her head. "It's just... It's nothing. I feel like Kahr would love to tell you all about our relationship when we get back."

Noreena narrowed her eyes, her gaze roaming over Zaharra's face. "All right. So, how are those socks coming?"

Zaharra grabbed the socks, thankful for the change in topic. "They are dry enough. Here." She handed Noreena hers before putting her own socks on. Next were the boots, which Zaharra shoved her feet in with more force than she probably needed. "I think we should keep moving. I don't know about you, but I'm not feeling tired. Do we need to sleep in the goddess's realm?"

Noreena hesitated before shaking her head. "No, I don't think so. If I am remembering the stories correctly, it never mentioned sleeping. Zaharra, if I overstepped in asking—"

Zaharra got up quickly, stomping on the small flames to put out the fire before kicking the ashes over the remaining embers. "We should get going. Movement will warm up our bodies more than any fire would, anyway. The night sky is clear as can be. The moon should be enough to light our path."

She bent over to gather up the pieces of rope that had bound them together for a time. In the end, she had to cut them free, severing the rope into a few different pieces because they were too waterlogged to free the knots. They had used a bit of the rope to get the fire going, but besides that, Zaharra thought she could salvage what was left by tying the pieces together. She wasn't willing to leave one of the few things they still had behind. Besides the rope, they had two boot knives between them. The travel pack was long gone, lost to the river.

Noreena stood with her and pushed her hands inside her coat. "There is enough light, and if we hurry, we should get to the goddess's temple by daybreak."

Change

THE SOUND OF LIGHT knocking woke him up, and Kahr groaned, moving his head from the crook of Zaharra's neck. The first thing he noticed was the steady beat of her pulse, followed by the fact she was warm. Warm enough for a bead of sweat to roll down her forehead.

Relief blossomed through his chest as he glanced over to see Orina waking up to the knocking as well. "How is Noreena doing?"

Orina nodded. "She is warm. I'm not sure if we helped, but they are okay for now. I don't see any more injuries. But there could be more under their clothes."

Kahr grimaced.

He hadn't thought of that. Of course, they could have gotten hurt in the way of bruises, sprains, and breaks under their clothing and he wouldn't even know.

"Should we... check?"

The words felt wrong the moment they left his mouth, and Orina shook her head. "There is nothing we can do. When they get to the temple, the goddess will bless them. Her blessing should heal any mortal wounds, or so the stories go."

Kahr rubbed his eyes and growled softly as the knocking continued. "Whatever could they need?"

"I don't know," Orina whispered. "But you should probably check, because I don't think they will stop."

"You might just be right."

"If you trust me, I can stay and watch."

He sighed and rubbed at his face again. He wasn't sure when his mind had changed, but somehow Kahr knew he could trust Orina to keep watch over Zaharra and his sister. "Promise me, if anything, anything at all changes, you will send Ari to get me immediately. No one else comes in here while I'm away."

"Agreed."

Kahr leaned over to kiss Zaharra on the temple. "I'll be back."

He moved silently not to disturb the elder and Ari, who were both sleeping next to the fire. He wasn't sure how they hadn't woken up, but he also didn't put too much thought into it. Let them sleep. There wasn't anything any of them could do but sit and wait.

Kahr reached for the door and pulled it open, cursing softly as the morning light blinded him. Throwing up his arm to shield his eyes, he blinked away the lingering bright spots before focusing on who was disturbing them.

It was the young boy, the one from yesterday, who had run to announce their presence. In his hands, he held a basket, which he put at Kahr's feet. "My mom told me to bring this to you. Said our clan leader might be hungry."

Kahr looked down at the basket.

It was modestly filled with a water jug, a loaf of bread, along with some wrapped cheese, and a couple of steaming sweet potatoes. "Tell your mother thank—"

The kid took off at a dead run before Kahr could finish, and he chuckled under his breath.

"Kids will be kids." A low voice came from the left, and Kahr turned to see a goliath man, looking to be in his fifties, holding a couple of steaming mugs. "My wife told me to give you this." He held out the mugs. "It's coffee, the good stuff traded in from the port city. Orina always stopped by in the mornings to get some for herself and Noreena."

"Thanks," Kahr murmured as he took the two mugs. "Noreena isn't... She hasn't..."

"Woken yet? That's to be expected. The second coffee is for you or the elder, if you don't want it."

"Right, I…" He glanced at the hut door, then at the two mugs and the basket at his feet.

The goliath man laughed before grabbing the basket and reaching for the door.

"Here, let me help."

Kahr nodded in appreciation, heading towards the dais.

Orina smiled, accepting the mug of coffee, and inhaled deeply. "Yorwen, the coffee smells as spectacular as ever."

The goliath man chuckled and put the basket down. "Tervena sent her son to deliver this as well."

"Is that coffee I smell?" The elder's voice rang out, and Kahr turned, making his way to Mervian and held out the second mug. "You should go talk to the people. Make your presence known. They are probably worried about their clan leader."

"They don't know me. Why would they be worried?" Kahr asked as he sat down next to the elder.

"I wasn't talking about you. Your sister ran this clan for the last two years while your father was dying. Running the mountain was always for the benefit of the other clan leaders, not the clan itself. They already accepted her. Go show them that everything will be okay. Give them some reassurance."

"How can I give them reassurance when I don't even know if Noreena and Zaharra are going to make it?"

Mervian shrugged and slurped at her coffee. "You're the leader, not me."

"Thanks for the help." Kahr shook his head, sarcasm dripping from every word, but the elder was right. He was their clan leader, at least until Noreena's spirit returned. He needed to give the clan reassurance, which meant leaving this hut.

And leaving Zaharra's side.

Conflict warred inside of him but in the end, he knew what Zaharra would tell him to do.

"Yorwen," he called out, and the goliath man turned away from his conversation with Orina.

"Yes?"

"Would it be too bold to ask you to walk me around the camp? So I can re-familiarize myself?" Kahr asked.

Yorwen smiled. "I thought you would never ask! Of course I would love to. The people have been waiting to meet you all night."

The camp had changed little in the setup since he had been away, yet everything felt different. He could see the subtle changes in the way everyone interacted. He had told Zaharra that there were distinct gender roles within Goliath culture. How the women weren't treated as equals to the men, yet everywhere he looked he could see how the elder was right. His sister had been changing things.

The change was subtle yet staggering, and for the hundredth time today, he was awestruck by how the clan's people loved his sister. In every interaction they asked about her, they asked about Zaharra, and they wanted to know what they could do to help him.

His sister was truly loved by her people.

Because that was what they were.

Her people.

He was sitting in Yorwen's small family hut, lost in thought, when a steaming mug of coffee slid into his view.

Yorwen's wife, Lowinda, sat down with a soft smile. "A coffee for your thoughts."

Kahr smiled and accepted the offering. "I was just thinking about how much the clan loves Noreena and is so willing to accept her as their leader, even though she is a woman."

Lowinda raised an eyebrow, and Kahr felt like a child with his hand caught in a honey jar.

"I mean... I didn't mean it like that. I know women can lead. I live among orcs, and they are matrilineal, and Zaharra..."

Lowinda laughed and shook her head, reaching out to pat Kahr's forearm. "I know what you meant.

Goliaths have never had a clan leader who was a woman. But we aren't the same people you left all those years ago. The change is subtle, but it is still change. You can see it in some of the other clans too, Thoreston's for example. He is hoping to have one of his daughters take his place as well. But there are others who oppose it."

"Like Hunter?" Kahr blurted out.

Lowinda nodded. "Yes, like Hunter and the other two young leaders, who he spends his time with. They don't want the change your sister brings with her. They don't care about their people the way your sister cares about us."

"What if the goddess doesn't bless her?"

It was a question weighing on his heart, one he had been thinking about all night.

"Does she really need the goddess's blessing?"

Kahr glanced at Lowinda as she grasped his hand in hers.

"Your sister is the leader we need, whether the goddess blesses her or not. If she would have asked us, we would have told her, fuck running the mountain. She has been leading us for years. Even before your father got sick. The people know a natural leader when we see one."

Kahr sucked in a breath, not knowing what to say to such a confession, when the door to the hut flew open, and Yorwen stumbled in.

"Hurry, come quick!"

Ruins of a Temple

MORNING LIGHT TRICKLED THROUGH the greying night sky, casting an eerie but beautiful glow around them as Zaharra and Noreena crested the mountaintop. The ruins of a temple under partial covers of snow came into view, and Zaharra stopped, catching her breath.

"Is that... Is that the goddess Wylder's temple?" Zaharra coughed before wincing. Her ribs and back still ached and climbing the side of a mountain was not helping any.

"Mmmm, yes." Noreena seemed hesitant in answering, and Zaharra glanced her way.

"What's wrong?"

"I don't know. It just feels too easy. Besides yesterday, doesn't it feel like I should have been tested more? I'm here to show I can be a leader, and I don't feel like..." Noreena curled her lip slightly, glancing around as if expecting something or someone to jump them at any moment.

"You don't feel tested?" Zaharra huffed and straightened slightly, lifting her hands over her head.

Noreena squinted at her, putting a hand over her eyes to block out the rising sun. "Are you okay? You are wheezing."

"I'm fine. Just sore," Zaharra answered, perhaps a little too curtly before heading towards the direction of the temple.

She tested the steps.

The temple was in all sorts of disarray, but the steps held under her weight. That was good enough for her.

She sat down with a groan and leaned back, throwing her arms to the sides. Closing her eyes, she concentrated on her breathing. Her back spasmed for a brief moment and Zaharra winced.

A shadow crept over her face, and she peeked an eye open.

Noreena glared down at her, hands on her hips. "You're not fine. You got injured in the river, didn't you?"

"It's just a little bruising."

Her back spasmed again, nausea crawling up her spine this time, and Zaharra sucked in an involuntary breath, causing the pain in her ribs to blossom.

"Right." Noreena dropped to the steps. "Show me this light bruising. Lucky for you, Orina is a healer, and she imparted some of her skills onto me."

"It's..."

She was going to say fine again, brush off the pain, but the look on Noreena's face stopped her. Zaharra sighed and unbuttoned her outer coat and tossed it to the side. She started to lift her tunic, but stopped midway as her back cramped.

"Let me help," Noreena commanded and took over, getting Zaharra's top over her head.

She was left sitting there in only her breast wrap as Noreena's cold hands pressed against her back.

She hissed slightly, and Noreena tsked at her.

"Light bruising, my ass. I'm amazed you made it up the mountain without passing out. And the bruising on your ribs is suspicious. I think they might be broken."

"I've had broken ribs before. It hurt worse."

"Right," Noreena huffed and got up, meandering over to the crest of the mountain path.

Zaharra got up to follow. "Where are you—"

Noreena waved her off before bending over and grabbing the leaves of some greenish blue plant.

Zaharra settled back down, letting the morning light wash over her as a breeze echoed from somewhere within the crumbling temple. She glanced around, Noreena's worry about this being a little too easy gnawing at her gut.

She was right.

Besides yesterday, it seemed like all the testing was directed towards Zaharra, and she most definitely did not want to be clan leader. All she wanted was to get her spirit back into her body and her body back into Kahr's arms.

Noreena moseyed back to her, hands full of shiny thick leaves, which she laid down on the step next to Zaharra. Holding one up, she broke it in half. It oozed and let off a deep, earthy scent.

"It's called Stinging Holly. Burns and causes vomiting if ingested, but if you put the inside sap on bruises and cuts..." Noreena spread the plant's sap along Zaharra's lower back, and she sucked in a deep breath. The relief was almost immediate, her back feeling cool and numb at the same time. "It releases the tension in muscles and helps with inflammation." Noreena continued. She reached for another leaf and broke it, putting more of the sap on Zaharra's back and reaching her ribs.

Within a minute, she could take a full breath. Her back had stopped spasming and Zaharra slumped forward with a relieved sigh.

"You should have mentioned something earlier. We have been passing bushes of Stinging Holly for the last few miles."

"Sorry," Zaharra murmured. "I didn't want to slow us down."

"Well, it doesn't matter, anyway. The goddess isn't going to show herself." Noreena sighed. "I'm not getting her blessing as clan leader."

"Mmmm..." Zaharra sighed, basking in the numbness of her back, before sitting upright and turning towards Noreena, eyebrows pinching together. "I'm sorry. What did you just say?"

"If the goddess was going to bless me for clan leadership, she would be here at her temple. It's over."

Zaharra shook her head and grabbed her tunic, tugging it over her head and standing up. "No, we must have missed something. And maybe there is another temple. Maybe this, this doubt you have right now, *is* the test."

Noreena's breath hitched, a sad smile forming on her face. "You're sweet, but we are in the right place. There is no other temple. It's over. I failed, and I'll probably never know why, but I'll live with it, somehow. There is no other alternative."

Zaharra sat back down, and clenched her jaw as she stared at her feet. "I know all about failure."

She felt Noreena's eyes on her, and Zaharra continued. "I'm a... I'm a legacy. Right now, I should be in the queen's personal guard. Just like my mother was, and my grandmother, and her mother before her. I passed every test, but in the end, the queen looked at me, and she must have seen it somehow. I questioned if I actually wanted to be a queen's guard. Just the smallest sliver of doubt and…" Zaharra took a deep breath before placing her head in her hands, her voice muffled. "I think I'm glad I didn't pass. Gods, I've been wrestling with that feeling for a while now. Because I know that if I had passed, I would have never met Kahr. I would never have met you. I would never be here, sitting on the steps of a ruined temple in a goddess's realm. Never in my wildest dreams did I think any of this would happen."

Noreena squeezed her shoulder as tears dripped down Zaharra's face.

Lifting her head, she choked out a pathetic laugh. "I think what I'm trying to say is, maybe failure is a good thing? Maybe for you not being blessed by the goddess will put you on an adventure you could never have dreamed of? I mean, so what if you're blessed? No one else in clan leadership is. They were just lucky enough to be born into a bloodline that once, a long time ago, was picked by the goddess. A bloodline that you share, by the way. The only difference is that they are men and you are a woman. So, what if you go back and just be a clan leader? Kahr would happily relinquish leadership to you. He does not want it. Trust me, we were trying to figure out ways to get him out of it on the way up the mountain."

Noreena sighed and scratched at her head. "I love your optimism, and I agree with you about the bloodlines. The issue is, if I don't get blessed by the goddess Wylder herself, the other clan leaders will dismiss my leadership. My people won't follow me, and all the change I want to bring about won't happen."

"So, that's it then? You just... give up? All of this, everything we just went through, was for nothing?" Zaharra asked.

"I mean, I wouldn't say nothing. We had some girl-on-girl bonding time." Noreena chuckled and nudged Zaharra with her shoulder.

"What makes you think your people wouldn't follow you?"

A voice, sounding both ethereal and terrifying, echoed out from deep within the temple.

Blessing

THEY TURNED AT THE same time towards the entrance of the temple as a woman with skin the color of stars emerged from the darkness. Her long midnight blue hair tumbled over her shoulders and down her back in waves, and Zaharra sucked in a breath as piercing grey eyes met hers.

The woman stepped into the morning light, and Zaharra threw her hand up to cover her eyes as the woman's skin reflected the light.

"Oh, shoot. I forgot you mortals have such sensitive eyes," the woman's voice thundered, and Zaharra dropped her arm as the light dimmed.

She glanced at the sky to see clouds covering the sun. The woman's skin still glowed, but it was bearable now. Zaharra glanced to the side as Noreena gaped at the woman in front of them.

"Wylder... is this... is it..." Noreena stuttered and glanced at Zaharra. "Is the goddess of the mountain and winter herself in front of us? Is this real?"

Zaharra nodded, wide-eyed, as the goddess laughed, the ground beneath the temple rumbling slightly.

"Yes, my young ones. I apologize for making you wait. It has been some time since mortal spirits have ventured into my realm," Wylder said before getting closer. Her bare feet made no sound as she circled them both. "Oh Fate, you truly have outdone yourself this time," she murmured.

The goddess made a full circle, putting herself in front of Zaharra and Noreena once more. She cocked her head and set her appraising eyes on Zaharra.

"I see you and I apologize for testing you, but I had to make sure you could truly live up to your namesake as a Fairstone."

Zaharra stiffened as fur rubbed against her leg. The goddess outstretched her hand as a mountain leopard appeared seemingly out of nowhere. It nudged at Zaharra again before stalking forward and sitting at the goddess's feet.

"There you are, Kita." The goddess glanced at Noreena with a smirk. "Did you still want to pet the kitty?"

A snort escaped before Zaharra slapped her hand against her mouth, silencing her laughter. Her body shook as a mortified look overcame Noreena.

"I... um, I..." Noreena stammered and glanced between the leopard, the goddess, and Zaharra.

Another snort escaped Zaharra, her eyes watering, and Noreena scowled at her. "It's not funny."

"It's a little funny," both the goddess and Zaharra said at the same time.

Wylder smiled and shook her head. "Alright. Enough games. You came to be blessed, did you not?"

Noreena nodded and her eyebrows crinkled, a look of worry overcoming her face.

"And yet, you don't feel worthy, do you? You said I haven't tested you?"

Zaharra held her breath as the goddess stepped forward and brushed the hair from Noreena's face, tucking it behind her hair.

"I've been testing you for a long time, Noreena Roakheart. Longer than you could even know. I picked you because you have a quiet strength buried deep inside. You have always pushed back against the norms, you always questioned. You will make an excellent leader, and your people know this. You've never needed my blessing. I wish you could have seen that before coming here. They would follow without hesitation if you had just asked them, but I will give my blessing, regardless."

The goddess leaned forward, pressing her lips against Noreena's forehead.

Zaharra sucked in a deep breath as a pale blue light glowed, a small rune left behind on Noreena's forehead as the goddess pulled away.

"And you." She turned towards Zaharra and gripped her hand. Light pulsed from the goddess's hands, making its way from Zaharra's wrist to her elbow. As the light faded, it left behind a pattern of delicate swirls and runes.

"Our newest clan leader will need a guard. And who is better equipped than a legacy? Someone whose bloodline has put queens upon thrones." The goddess took a step back, a soft smile etched upon her face. "Change is upon us. Goliath kind will step into a new future. I am looking forward to seeing how far you will go. Both of you."

Zaharra reached out, grasping at Noreena's hand as a fine mist began to encapsulate the goddess and her temple. Magic poured around them, and she closed her eyes as she felt her spirit go weightless.

"They are back!" Ari's shrill yell echoed out as Zaharra blinked her eyes open. She was greeted by a darkened room, the sound of a fire crackling in the vicinity. Anxiety blossomed through her chest for a moment as she tried to get a bearing on her surroundings.

She sat up with a groan and rubbed at her temples as Ari zipped around her head a few times.

"Tell me everything! Was it epic? Did you slay any monsters? Did you see the goddess? Did—"

"Ari!" the elder's voice snapped. "Give them a moment to breathe."

Zaharra silently thanked the elder. She was still trying to process their encounter with the goddess Wylder, and being chosen to be Noreena's guard. What did this mean for her?

And for Kahr?

She frowned and looked around.

Speaking of which...

"Zaharra, how is your back? The cut on my forehead is gone," Noreena's low voice echoed out, and she turned to see her sitting next to another goliath woman.

"I'm Orina," the goliath woman squeaked as Noreena pulled her into her lap.

"Oh, Orina, it's nice to meet you. Noreena told me about you," Zaharra murmured as she shrugged off her outercoat and lifted her shirt slightly. She looked at her ribs and turned. "Nothing hurts anymore. What about my back?"

"The goddess healed you. Healed you both when she blessed you. Just like the stories said she would." Orina laughed as she struggled to get out of Noreena's hold.

Zaharra blushed slightly and looked away, giving the couple a moment alone. She met the stares of a very put-out fairy hovering in front of her and an elder who wore a slight smirk.

"Where's Kahr?" she asked, her voice slightly cracking. While she knew he had a clan to take care of, Zaharra still wished he would have been there when she woke up.

"Don't be so sad, young one." The elder scoffed. "We had to pry Kahr away from your side this morning to make an appearance to the clan. The people needed a little reassurance. He has only been gone for a few hours. Go to him."

Zaharra glanced over her shoulder and snorted, before glancing away. Noreena and Orina were in a full-on make-out session.

Best to leave them to it then.

She got up with a slight groan and headed towards the door, Ari and the elder following on her heels. Pushing open the door, she grimaced as the morning light hit her eyes and threw her arm up to help with the glare.

As she stepped outside, an older goliath man met her eyes, and surprise drifted across his face before he took off at a sprint and slammed open a door a few huts down.

"Hurry, come quick!" the man's voice bellowed, and Zaharra smiled as Kahr emerged.

Kahr's eyes widened, and within a single breath, he was in front of her, falling to his knees to wrap his strong arms around her waist. His swift movement threw her off balance, and she laughed as they both fell into a tangled heap.

"Sweetheart, fuck, I should have been there when you woke up. I'm so sorry. Forgive me," Kahr whispered as he peppered her face with kisses.

Zaharra tangled her hands into Kahr's disheveled hair and found his lips with hers, kissing him hard. He groaned into her mouth, and after a few moments, she broke the kiss, pulling back slightly. "There is nothing to be sorry about. You're here now. That's all that matters."

Kahr brushed the hair out of her face, kissing her softly on the lips again.

A small gasp echoed out above them, and Zaharra glanced up to see a crowd had gathered. She blushed before noticing they weren't focused on her but on the door of the hut.

She turned her head at the same time as Kahr to see Noreena had emerged, Orina by her side.

Sunlight glinted off the glowing pale blue rune tattooed on Noreena's forehead. A throbbing pulse echoed through Zaharra's arm, and she glanced down to see that her tattoo was also glowing.

"Your new clan leader and her guard have both returned. A celebration we must have this very night!" The elder's voice rang out, and the crowd cheered.

Zaharra met Kahr's eyes and smiled hesitantly. "We should probably have a talk. I don't think we will be leaving the clan any time soon."

"No need, sweetheart. I'm by your side, no matter what. As long as you will have me," he murmured, rubbing his nose against hers.

Zaharra giggled and wrapped her arms around Kahr as he stood, bringing her with him.

"Of course I will have you." She laughed, yelling out to Kahr as the crowd of goliaths descended around Noreena and her, lifting them both up into the air in celebration.

Stargazing

WATER LAPPED AT KAHR'S shins as he sat on the smooth rocks surrounding the natural hot springs. Zaharra sat between his legs, facing away as he worked his fingers across her tight shoulders.

She groaned as he found a knot and began massaging it.

Delighted shouts and rambunctious laughter of the party celebrating Noreena as the new clan leader echoed through the night air. The party had been going full swing since mid-afternoon. Based on the position of the stars, they were closing in on the next day.

But the celebration wasn't just for Noreena becoming clan leader. It was also celebrating her engagement to Orina, and that new times were among them.

Noreena was going to bring change to the clan, and hopefully others. It would be a long road ahead, but their people were excited.

Noreena even had a handful of women interested in becoming part of her guard.

A task set upon Zaharra by the goddess Wylder herself.

His gaze dropped to the swirling tattoo decorating her right arm. The runes intertwined in the delicate swirls were the same as the one that adorned his sister's forehead.

Kahr moved on from Zaharra's shoulders, and his thoughts as he threaded his hands through her hair.

Zaharra's breath hitched as he massaged her scalp, and she leaned back to stare up at him.

He curled down to press a soft kiss to her lips, and the water splashed as she reached up to grab his face.

Kissing her long and tenderly, he nipped at her bottom lip and sucked on it. She moaned in his mouth, her hands sliding from his face to tangle into his hair.

He slid a hand down to collar her throat and tugged at her hair to lean her head back even farther.

Her whimper set his blood on fire, his cock hard and aching. But there would be time for that later. Right now, all he wanted to do was pleasure his woman.

Kahr broke the kiss and stood up, moving around Zaharra to stand in front of her. Her lust-hazed eyes roamed his naked body, and she bit her bottom lip. Leaning in, he braced his hands on either side of her body.

"There is something I've been dying to do to you," he growled as Zaharra reached out, her fingers trailing over his lower abs and hipbones.

"Oh, and what is that?"

His cock twitched at her breathy words, and her eyes immediately focused downwards. Her hand trailed over his cock, fingertips drifting over his piercings.

His cock twitched again as she wrapped her hand around it before leaning in, and Kahr sucked in a sharp breath as Zaharra used the tip of her tongue, licking the big vein in his cock from base to tip.

She looked up at him with her big, beautiful amber eyes, and Kahr groaned, low in his throat. "That... you can do that later, sweetheart. It's my turn to taste you."

Kahr reached down, wrapping his arms around Zaharra's waist, and lifted her out of the water.

She giggled as he put her down on the towel he had been sitting on earlier and pushed her into a laying position.

"I guess I'll just lie back and watch the stars then." Zaharra chuckled, and Kahr shook his head with a smile before getting to his knees and throwing her legs over his shoulders. He dipped his head and kissed her inner thighs, his hands tightening on her hips as Zaharra gasped and grabbed his hair.

"Kahr." His name came out strangled from Zaharra's throat as he trailed his lips across her inner thighs, before licking her pussy in one long stroke.

Her hold on his hair tightened, Zaharra's hips bucking into him as he continued his long, teasing strokes.

"Oh fuck," Zaharra whimpered, and Kahr thrust his tongue inside of her, one hand trailing over her hips to play with her clit.

She gasped and her thighs shook as Kahr felt the inner walls of Zaharra's pussy flutter around his tongue.

Growling, he pulled her closer, kissing his way up her stomach to her chest. Her legs fell from his shoulders, hitching lazily around his hips.

"How's the stargazing going, sweetheart?" Kahr murmured as he flicked the tip of Zaharra's hard nipple with his tongue.

"Mmmm, it's going great," Zaharra moaned and panted before arching her back, turning Kahr on even more.

His cock throbbed, and Zaharra lifted her hips in response. All he had to do was push forward, his head of his cock resting at her slick entrance, and he would be inside of her.

But Kahr had a much better position in mind.

He leaned up, the head of his cock slipping away from Zaharra's slick entrance and smirked as her gaze sharpened and caught his. Her legs tightened around his waist as she narrowed her eyes at him.

"And just where do you think you are going?"

"Turn around and slide back into the water," Kahr whispered as he stroked her legs.

Zaharra bit her bottom lip as she unhooked her legs and turned around, doing just as he asked. She turned to look at him over her shoulder, and Kahr wrapped a hand around the front of her neck, lifting her chin and kissing her.

The water lapped around their thighs as he pressed his chest into her back and grabbed her by the waist, lifting her hips. His cock slid against her entrance, and Zaharra whimpered in his mouth. She reached back to tangle a hand in his hair as Kahr used his thigh to spread her legs wider.

Kahr broke the kiss and nibbled his way across her jaw. He leaned forward slightly, not enough to bend Zaharra over completely, but just enough to plant his other hand onto the edge of the smooth stone surrounding the hot springs.

The tip of his cock aligned perfectly with Zaharra's pussy, and he pressed his hips forward as she pressed hers back.

Her mewling moan sent a shiver down his spine as he sank halfway into her. "That's it, sweetheart,"

Kahr whispered into her ear as he shifted his hips a little more, sliding in a few more inches. "You're taking me so well."

"Fuck," Zaharra groaned, her hand tightening in his hair as she turned her head to let it rest on his shoulder.

Kahr moved the hand around her neck to cup her chin, his lips caressing hers as he continued rocking his hips.

Zaharra's breath hitched, her gasps turning to pants as Kahr tightened his hold on her. He clenched his jaw and moaned low in his throat as he continued his slow, grinding thrusts. He felt her tightening around him, and a moment later, she came with a breathless scream. She went weightless in his arms as Kahr felt his cock strain and twitch, her pussy still pulsating around him as he came with her.

Their ragged breathing filled the air as Kahr kissed the side of Zaharra's neck, making his way towards her mouth, and pressed a featherlight kiss to her lips.

He pulled his hips back slowly, and Zaharra mumbled something he didn't quite catch. Running his hand down her spine, he fully slipped out of her and grabbed her by the hips, turning Zaharra around to face him. "What was that, sweetheart?"

She wrapped her arms around his neck and laid her head in the crook of his neck and shoulder as he grabbed her hips and lifted her legs out of the water. With her legs around his waist, she mumbled again.

"I don't want nights like this to end."

Kahr pressed a kiss to her forehead as he walked them out of the hot springs and over to their clothes and towels. "They never will for as long as you will have me, Zaharra."

"Forever then?" she whispered, and Kahr sat her down on the bench, wrapping a towel around her.

He cupped her face and kissed her softly. "If that's how long you will have me, then yes, forever. "

She smiled and kissed him back harder. "We should probably get back to the party."

Kahr shrugged. "Or... or we can go back to our sleeping hut and ... sleep."

He winked, and Zaharra laughed before getting to her feet and grabbing their clothes. "Ahhh, yes, I think I am very... sleepy."

She grinned before taking off at a full run, with only her towel on. Kahr shouted her name in surprise, before smirking and chasing after her.

Runs in the Family

Distant shouting startled Zaharra from her blissful sleep, and she grumbled, shifting over to snuggle into the warmth of Kahr's embrace. She swore she had only shut her eyes, and it was way too early to be waking up after what Kahr and she had done after getting back from the hot springs.

The shouting became louder, and Zaharra grumbled again as Kahr shook her slightly.

"Zaharra, you need to wake up."

His deep voice sounded strained, and Zaharra opened her eyes.

"What is..." She paused mid-sentence as the shouting became clear.

Orc.

Whoever was shouting was saying "orc."

Zaharra scrambled out of bed as fast as she could, throwing on a pair of pants and a long-sleeve tunic.

Kahr was right behind her as she shoved the door to the sleeping hut open. An overcast day greeted her, along with a sight Zaharra's mind had trouble processing.

"Where is my daughter!" Zaharra's mother yelled, her voice booming through the quiet morning air.

"Mom?" Zaharra whispered as she stood frozen in the doorway.

Her mother's eyes snapped towards her as if she had yelled instead of whispered.

Zaharra met her mother's eyes and gripped the door to the hut even harder. She wanted to run to her mother like a child, but stopped herself. Her mother wouldn't be here looking for her unless something bad had happened.

"Did something... Is everyone all right?" Zaharra choked out as she pushed herself away from the door and took a shaking step towards her mother.

"No." Her mother's normally authoritative voice quivered, and she strode forward, throwing her arms around Zaharra.

The hug startled her, her breath catching. Oh gods, something terrible had happened.

"No," her mother said again, holding her tighter. "You left. You left and I couldn't let you think..."

Zaharra blinked in confusion as her mother pulled back and gripped her face, looking into her eyes.

"Meerek stopped by the farm a few days ago. She told me you had left. And I.... I just couldn't let you leave thinking I was mad. We have had our fights before, we both have a stubborn streak a mile long, but you... you've never left before, and it broke me. Zaharra, my baby, I'm sorry. I don't care that you're not following in the family's footsteps. I'll stand by any decision you make, just never leave again without saying goodbye. And I'm sorry how I handled you coming back from the city with the news that you wouldn't be in the queen's guard. It was a shock, and I struggled with it. But it doesn't matter. I am not disappointed in you, and I love you. Just please never run away like this again."

"Wait," Zaharra shook her head and lifted her hands to grab her mother's, which still cupped her face. "You came all the way up the mountain... all by yourself? To tell me you loved me?

"Seems to run in the family," Kahr voice echoed out from behind her.

Zaharra watched as her mother's eyes snapped over her shoulder and narrowed like a predator seeing its prey.

Her mother took a step back and cocked her head. "It seems like that, doesn't it, Trader? I've seen you around town. Why did my daughter follow you up these mountains?"

"Because I love him." The words fell from her lips before Zaharra could contain them. She glanced over her shoulder at Kahr. His eyes met hers, his face softening as he swept her up in a hug from behind.

Everything around her seemed to disappear as Kahr placed his hand on her cheek and smiled softly. "I love you too."

"I'm not sharing my wedding day with my brother." Noreena's sarcastic voice brought Zaharra back to reality.

"And you are?" Zaharra's mother asked.

"Noreena, new clan leader. What do you want with my guard?"

Zaharra's mother's eyes widened, her eyebrows lifting to her hairline.

Surprise.

It was a look she hadn't seen on her mother's face in a long time.

"Guard? My daughter is your guard?"

"Mom, a lot... a lot has happened in the last few days," Zaharra butted in and rolled up the sleeve to her tunic, showing the markings the goddess had left behind.

Her mother glanced between the markings on her arm and the matching rune on Noreena's forehead.

"Those are the markings of the goddess Wylder," Zaharra's mother whispered before shaking her head. "But I thought goliaths did not let women into leadership roles. How are you the clan leader?"

"Like Zaharra said, a lot has happened." Noreena glanced at her and smiled. "I am happy the goddess picked you. Even if I have to put up with you kissing my brother. It's gross, by the way."

Zaharra scoffed and rolled her eyes before doing just that and leaning back into Kahr for another kiss.

He grunted in surprise before kissing her back.

It was a quick kiss, just a few seconds, but Zaharra smiled as Noreena made gagging noises behind her.

"We will talk about *that* later." Her mother's deadpan voice rang out, and Zaharra glanced to the ground quickly, warmth rolling over her cheekbones. She peeked up to see her mom shake her head before turning her attention to Noreena.

"Being a guard is a sacred duty in our family, and I'm positive Zaharra will not let you down, but she is only one person. Do you have any other guards, or is this something new? What type of training needs to be conducted?"

Zaharra bit her lip, trying to hide her smile from the excited tone she caught in her mother's voice.

"It's new. There are a few goliaths who have spoken to me already. Those who are interested. Women and men," Noreena answered before glancing over Zaharra's mother's shoulder.

Zaharra followed her gaze to see an older goliath dressed in clan leader furs, walking up the path slowly. He had been at the meeting before, in the hut. He was one of the few who outright supported Noreena becoming a clan leader.

He paused, glancing at Kahr before lowering his head in Noreena's direction. "I'm sorry I missed the celebration. I didn't want to intrude, but I wanted to make sure Ninie made it here. She ended up in my village first, and I gave her directions."

"Thoreston, you're never an intrusion!" Noreena yelled in excitement and rushed forward, holding out her arms.

Zaharra felt Kahr's whole body stiffen, and she glanced up at him, seeing his face harden. "Do we not like this clan leader?" she whispered.

Kahr shook his head and closed his eyes. "Yes, no. It's complicated."

She reached up and cupped his face. "Is Noreena safe around him, or do I need to kick his ass?"

Kahr snorted, and his lips twitched into a half smile. "It's fine. No ass-kicking needed."

"Good," Zaharra's mother interjected, having moved to her side to watch the interaction between the two clan leaders. "Because if he was a danger, then you are already failing at being her guard."

"Mom!" Zaharra whined. "I have this under control."

"Mmhhhm, I'm sure you do, but there is still a lot that needs to be done here," her mom said. "Starting a guard unit from the ground up takes a lot of work."

Zaharra sighed and crossed her arms. "I know that, Mom. You taught me everything I needed to know to be a queen's guard. And I was going to send you a letter asking for help. Even *I* know I need it."

Zaharra's mom glanced around the village and nodded. "There is a lot of work to be done. We should get started."

Her mother walked past them, farther into the village as Zaharra gawked after her. "Wait, what? What do you mean? Like right now? Mom... Mom, get back here."

One Year Later

ZAHARRA GIGGLED AS KAHR swung her in a wide circle, before pulling her back into his embrace, holding her tightly against him. They swayed to the music, and Zaharra sighed, leaning her head against his shoulder.

Her cheeks hurt from smiling all day, but she couldn't stop.

She didn't want to stop.

Her marriage to Kahr happened earlier in the day at the town square, and the whole village, along with a handful of goliaths from Noreena's clan, had attended.

It had been overwhelming and amazing at the same time, and the party after the ceremony had been rambunctious.

Early day had fallen to late afternoon as the party died down into a more intimate affair back at her parents' house. Her family, and Meerek, along with Noreena and her wife, Orina, plus Ari. The little fairy was the first to pass out and was currently snoring away on Orina's lap.

The clearing of a man's voice had Zaharra turning in Kahr's arms, and her eyes widened as her brother Dalin stood in the backyard, the sun setting behind him.

Zaharra squealed as the rest of the family jumped from their chairs and rushed forward.

"Brother! You're back."

Zaharra ran forward and wrapped her arms around her brother in a tight hug.

He chuckled and patted her on her back before dropping his bag and hugging the rest of the family.

"We weren't expecting you back so soon," Zaharra's father grunted as he pulled Dalin into a tight hug.

"Same, same..." Dalin said before pulling away and adjusting his glasses. He gulped before taking a step back. "I ... I don't want you all to overreact."

Zaharra narrowed her eyes, and her mother took a step forward, arms crossed. "Well, I would say you did something fucking stupid, but you're the one child I never had to worry about that with. So, spill."

Dalin cleared his throat and turned to look over his shoulder. "You can come out. I told you, you didn't have to wait."

Zaharra's eyes widened as a delicate elven woman, who was at least a foot shorter than her brother, stepped into view. Her sparkling green eyes roamed over everyone as she silently padded up to Dalin's side and flashed a hesitant smile. She rested her fingers on Dalin's arm, and he gulped slightly before adjusting his glasses.

A classic sign that her brother was nervous.

Zaharra glanced between her brother and the woman at his side. Kahr's arm that was wrapped around her waist tightened, pulling her in closer.

"Well, come on, introduce us. I don't know why you are being so awkward." Zaharra laughed and reached forward to grab the woman's hand. "Not sure why my brother is being so weird. If you are dating, it's totally fine. I'm Zaharra, by the way, and this..." she paused to wave over her shoulder, "is Kahr. Welcome to our after-wedding party."

The woman blushed slightly and took Zaharra's hand. She shook it in a greeting Zaharra wasn't akin to, but she didn't mind.

Dalin cleared his throat again. "We aren't dating."

"Okay, then. Does 'we are not dating' have a name?"

Their mother cleared her throat, and Zaharra glanced her way. She was giving Dalin a look Zaharra knew meant trouble was coming if someone didn't give her clarification right at this moment.

The look seemed to knock some sense into her brother, and Dalin took a deep breath and squared his shoulders back.

"Liza, I would like you to meet my family."

"See, that wasn't so hard," Zaharra said, "Liza, welcome."

Her brother met her eyes, and Zaharra's jaw dropped as his next words knocked the wind out of her.

"Family, I would like you to meet my wife."

Dear Reader

Dear Reader
First off,
Thank you so much for giving Violet Fields &
Midnight Mountains a chance.
I hope you enjoyed the love story between Zaharra
and Kahr, as much as I loved writing it.
And if it isn't to much trouble, reviews are what
make the amazon algorithm put my stories in front
of other who might enjoy it too.
Secondly,
I'm sorry for the tiny cliffhanger at the end of the
book!
I'll be honest with you though; I really want
you to pick up book two (as this is a series of
interconnected standalones). So, I thought what
better way to introduce the main characters for the
second book?

Yes, you read that right. The second book will follow the love story of Zaharra's brother, Dalin and the mysterious elven woman, Liza.
Believe me, this is one you don't want to miss.
But in the meantime,
If you enjoyed Violet Fields & Midnight Mountains, be sure to check out some of my other work.
I think Fireworks in the Bayou or Snowflakes & Vampires Kisses would be right up your alley. Both are funny, sweet, yet deliciously spicy short stories. And be sure to check out my *also by* page for more of my work.
Until next time,
Astrid Vail
PS:
You can follow me on my Amazon page to be in the know when any new releases drop.
Or if you are interested you can sign up for my mailing list at www.astridvail.com

Also by Astrid Vail

Wild Romance, Epic Adventure- Multi-Genre Romance writer
Mood Writing for Mood Readers
You can find my books at your favorite retailer and don't forget to visit me at www.astridvail.com
Wicked Fate, Lusty Mates
Carnal Moon: A Steamy M/F Paranormal Erotic Romance
Wild Moon: A Smoldering M/F Paranormal Erotic Romance
Enchanted Moon: A Second Chance M/F Paranormal Erotic Romance
Arctic Moon: A Sultry M/F Paranormal Erotic Romance
Feral Moon – A Seductive M/F Paranormal Erotic Romance

Scarlet Moon – A Spicy M/F Paranormal Erotic Romance

Fairytales After Dark

Claiming Jafar: A M/F Enemies to Lovers 'Villain gets the Girl' Fairytale

Gaston's Beast: An M/M Beauty and the Beast Retelling

Hunting Red: A F/F Red Riding Hood Reimagining

Princess Bound: A M/F Friends to Enemies to Lovers Second Chance Fairytale.

Wicked Snow: A 'Why Choose' Dark Romance Snow White Retelling

Holidays After Dark

Winter's Eve: A M/F Fantasy Holiday Short Story

Valentine's Arrow: A M/F Paranormal Holiday Short Story

Fireworks in the Bayou: A M/F Paranormal Holiday Short Story

Snowflakes and Vampire Kisses: A M/F Paranormal Holiday Short Story

Sugar and Spice Fantasy Romance

Violet Fields & Midnight Mountains: A M/F Cozy High Fantasy Romance

About My Pen Name

The first thing I would like to get out of the way is that, yes, Astrid Vail is a nom de plume. A pen name, if you will.

My true name is Dorothy Kilgore.

Why do I mention this?

Because in this day and age you can't be too careful, and I figured why not add one more duck in the row in case things go sideways and legal avenues ever need to be involved.

Plus, if I ever find my books in the bookstore, I will want to sign them, and this gives me an easy way of proving who I truly am.

When I first started publishing back in 2021, it was under the name DE Kilgore. I did not know what I was doing, like most newbie authors. After the first two books, I got in my head, poor advice outweighed the good, and after publishing two

full-length books and two longer novellas in two years…
I burned out.
Except I didn't know this and kept pushing myself. At the time of writing this, August 2025 - there are a good three half-written books sitting at 30k words in a world I do not know if I'll ever revisit again. The world and characters haunt me, in the best and worst of ways.
But back to my burnout in 2022 — I had to pivot, and in doing so I decided to just write. Write something for me and only me. Something that was not intended for public consumption.
The funny thing about burnout — at least mine — was I still had the ability to write. Yet, I became frozen because of the deadlines, from trying to force my characters into something the masses would love. I was trying to write for the market.
I was trying to change who I was as an author.
I listened to bad advice, and I rushed something that couldn't be rushed.
Writing is an art, and art should never be rushed. It should never be tamed into something palatable to the masses.
The rawer the art, the world, the characters — that is where I am most comfortable when writing.
No matter the story, light or dark, funny or heartbreaking, the stories you read from me as an

author are words pulled from the very recesses of my soul.

When I burned out, it was never the ideas, characters, or worlds. It was because I took those raw words and smothered their fire in fear of what the masses would think.

So, when I pivoted and decided to just write for myself, something I never expected was born.

Something I couldn't stop thinking about — something I realized I wanted to share with the world.

But fear is still a funny thing that gets under my skin from time to time, and I didn't really want anyone I knew to read what I wrote (at that time) so I decided, what about a pen name?

If the story fails, if it isn't received well... then we can just call it an experiment and move on.

And so, Astrid Vail was born.

From the darkness of burnout, Astrid pulled me back into my raw creative light.

Astrid was supposed to be my pen name for those little stories I felt were a little too dark — a little too raw to publish under my true name.

I told myself I would start writing again under DE Kilgore. That I would revisit the series I stopped and finish it out. And yet, every time I tried, I would fall back into the bad habits that led me to my burnout in the first place. I couldn't write what I wanted. I kept changing the characters into flat

renditions of who they truly were, and what was worse...
I knew what I was doing, and yet I could not stop.
Somewhere in the back of my mind, I thought these sweet characters and their epic quests couldn't be part of the Astrid Vail world.
What I didn't know then was that I was still trying to play the silly games and made-up rules that had led me to burnout in the first place.
Every time I felt myself teeter on the edge of burning out, I would open a new word doc and write something that would fall perfectly into the world of Astrid Vail.
Something raw and beautiful.
And every time I did, it felt like I could breathe again.
It took me some time to realize that the world of Astrid Vail wasn't only for those darker stories.
It took me a while to realize that Astrid Vail was not just my pen name, but my muse.
A muse born of my mind, from the darkest and rawest corner of my creative well.
When I finally realized this, I knew I could never publish under another name again.
The world of Astrid Vail embodies the rawest form of romance, and every subgenre that falls under the romance umbrella.
And it is a world where I have no plans of escaping anytime soon.